MW01077632

PARADISE ROT

PARADISE ROT

A Novel

JENNY HVAL

Translated by Marjam Idriss

VERSO

This translation has been published with the financial support of NORLA

This English-language edition first published by Verso 2018
First published as *Perlebryggeriet*
© Kolon Forlag 2009
Translation © Marjam Idriss 2018

Lyrics to 'Alison' reproduced by kind permission of
Neil Halstead and Cherry Red Songs

All rights reserved

The moral rights of the author have been asserted

9 10 8

Verso
UK: 6 Meard Street, London W1F 0EG
US: 20 Jay Street, Suite 1010, Brooklyn, NY 11201
versobooks.com

Verso is the imprint of New Left Books

ISBN-13: 978-1-78663-383-5
ISBN-13: 978-1-78663-384-2 (US EBK)
ISBN-13: 978-1-78663-385-9 (UK EBK)

British Library Cataloguing in Publication Data
A catalogue record for this book is available from the British Library

Library of Congress Cataloging-in-Publication Data

Names: Hval, Jenny, 1980– author. | Idriss, Marjam.
Title: Paradise rot : a novella / by Jenny Hval ; translated by Marjam Idriss.
Other titles: Perlebryggeriet. English
Description: London ; Brooklyn, NY : Verso, 2018.
Identifiers: LCCN 2018004566| ISBN 9781786633835
| ISBN 9781786633859 (UK EBK)
Classification: LCC PT8952.18.V35 P3713 2018 | DDC 839.823/8 – dc23
LC record available at https://lccn.loc.gov/2018004566

Typeset in Electra by Hewer Text UK Ltd, Edinburgh
Printed and bound by CPI Group (UK) Ltd, Croydon CR0 4YY

PARADISE ROT

Milk and Silk

THERE, AND NOT there.

Outside the hostel window the town is hidden by fog. The pier down below dissolves into the colourless distance, like a bridge into the clouds. At times the fog disperses a little, and the contours of islands appear a little way out to sea. Then they're gone again. *There, not there, there, not there*, I whisper, leaning against the window, drumming my fingers against the glass in time with the words, *dunk, du-dunk*, as if I'm programing a new heartbeat for a new home.

So I sat that first morning in Aybourne, leaning against the windowpane, forehead flat on the glass. My shoulders ached from carrying my backpack. I hadn't taken it off on the train from the airport. I just stood and held on tight to all my things while strange stations and billboards in bright colours whizzed past. The straps gnawed into my shoulders while I counted the stops to my destination. I studied how people would, instinctively, pull the handle to make the doors open at just the right time. I had tried to absorb the technique before it was my turn to get off, so that no one would realise this was my first time on this train. When the time came, however, I stood by the door and pulled the handle to no effect. A woman in her forties tapped my shoulder – *The other side, love* – and I just about managed to get off the train in time. After that I stood on the platform for a moment while a stream of rush-hour passengers passed me, like a river parting itself around a small rock.

The trip had been hard. I had too much luggage, my coat was too big, and I had become distressed in the duty-free shop, which was permeated by the smell of sickeningly sweet perfume. In the hostel my body became light and insubstantial, and I imagined that I, too, was being swallowed by fog, that I was dissolving in it. The remnants from my journey lay tossed around me: tickets and promotional leaflets on the table, an English fashion magazine on the bed, salt and pepper packets on the floor. The sound of cars on the street outside and a fly that buzzed under the curtains replaced the echo of that strange voice that had announced *doors closing* over the train's loudspeakers. I closed my eyes. The glass was cold and dry. When I stood up to take a shower, I had left a blurry oil-print on the pane.

The shared bathroom was across the hall. It was a dirty and colourless room with grey-yellow wallpaper and dark carpeted floors. The bathtub's enamel had faded and grown dull, and when I washed my hands there was no mirror over the sink, only a dark square impression and a rusted screw where a frame once hung. I found the mirror-glass on the cistern behind the toilet bowl, as if someone had used it to watch themself masturbate. Now it reflected my belly and hips, and I stood there like a man and unzipped my trousers with my front facing the toilet bowl. It felt almost strange not to have a dick to pull out through my fly. When I rolled my jeans and pants down my thighs, the dark triangle of pubic hair looked strangely empty, like a half-finished sketch. I turned around, sat down on the toilet seat and looked down between my legs, where a thin stream of urine trickled into the bowl. The dirty-white porcelain was tinged with acrid yellow. Almost a shame to flush away all that colour, I thought.

Afterwards I sat by a corner table in the breakfast hall. Breakfast was nearly over, and a bored waiter was stacking bowls filled with packets of cheese and jam in a refrigerator. A loud group of golfers sat nearby. Some of them had already put on caps and gloves, and they drank their coffee from paper cups with white-gloved hands. Long black golf bags were propped against the wall. The room was emptying and yet it felt full. The smell of the old smoky carpet mingled with the coffee. The sugar cubes in the bowl were covered in dust.

As I stepped out into the street, the morning light broke through the fog, catching on the tram tracks. I followed the tracks to the nearest stop, noting the trash on the pavement, a discarded juice carton and greasy pages of newsprint. My blurred reflection appeared in shop windows beneath unfamiliar English signs: *Newsagent*, *Chemist*, *Café*. When the tram came, that too bore a name I did not recognise, *Prestwick Hill*.

The carriage was half-full. Two rows of seats lined its sides, facing each other. A large inebriated man sat at the back, alternating between snoozing and babbling to himself. Every time he fell asleep, he slipped a little further off his seat. When he wriggled back into position, his oversized and low-riding trousers slipped a little further down his hips. He wasn't wearing anything underneath. The other passengers pretended not to notice. A few teens were chatting quietly, a girl read a magazine intently, and others stared out the window. I picked up my guidebook and turned the pages, but I couldn't concentrate. Like everyone else on the tram my attention was on the man and his trousers. Sometimes people would exchange quick glances, and when his trousers finally slipped past his hips and down his thighs, an uncomfortable sense of solidarity formed in the carriage, one common heart beating quickly and awkwardly. No one looked at the man, and yet every-one saw at once a flaccid red limb protruding from his crotch like a parched tongue. Agitation spread between the seats; our bodies started to itch and sweat. I looked around, and everywhere nervous glances met my own. Finally, two newly arrived men went over to the man, helped him put on his trousers again, and threw him politely out at the next stop. I saw him rave through the high street, carving a wide path in the crowd. The passengers in the carriage exhaled. They could return to themselves, disappear into their enclosures. I was alone again.

I got off the tram by a little park between big office buildings in the centre of town. The fog had finally lifted. Thick clouds were rushing far above my head, much higher and faster than the clouds at home, as if Aybourne were in a deep gorge. I had no plan and no map, so I sat down at a café and ordered what seemed easiest to pronounce. When my tea reached the table, they had put milk in the cup without asking, so much that the tea was completely white, but I didn't say anything. On the street outside, autumn rain had begun to fall. Between the businessmen with umbrellas and newspapers over their heads, the asphalt was dotted, dark grey and then black and gleaming like snail skin. I pulled my knees up in front of me on my chair, as if I sat in a little lifeboat drinking my white tea. I tried intermittently to read a newspaper, but my English wasn't up to it. Instead I watched the cars and listened to the rain through the open door. I listened to foot-steps and to raincoat fabric rubbing against skin and cotton when people sat; to strange heavy coins that jangled over by the counter and cups clattering against saucers.

When I returned to the hostel that afternoon, a tall Asian girl stood by the counter. She looked confused. The receptionist tried to explain how to check in. 'You need to sign your name here, please,' she said with a sigh, but the Asian girl didn't look like she quite under-stood. 'But I have a room, yes . . . From the university,' she said. A boy in a suit with an American accent tried to help, but the girl didn't understand him any better, and she looked tensely down at the counter. I tiptoed past them, happy to see other foreign students. There were more in the communal area: two girls from Montreal playing cards and a pair of siblings from Madagascar taking turns to use the phone. Later in the night I heard all four of them arguing loudly in French, and when one of them slammed a door, the floors creaked. The matted grey-blue carpet sent heavy dust clouds into the attic air.

Throughout the night an icy ocean wind blew through the cracked window, and I woke up the next morning feeling like the cold had sunk into me, turning bone to wood and skin to sawdust, making me like Pinocchio.

When I stretched, my shoulders creaked, and I put on several layers of thick clothes before leaving for breakfast.

The food in the breakfast hall was slippery and fluid: silky soft white bread slices that dissolved like candyfloss in my mouth. Glutinous jelly-like jam without seeds and of an uncertain berry flavour. Butter, smooth peanut butter, honey, milk, Marmite and ketchup. Soft rice puffs and soggy fried eggs. I remember everything at home as being textured: whole-wheat bread with hard crusts and coarse liver paste, the feeling of grains and fibrous meat swallowed with black tea, the whole lot going down your throat like wet gravel. Here, I chewed and only the sugar crunched. I sat poking a wet fingertip into the sugar bowl and then sucking on it, crushing the sugar crystals between my teeth.

The foreign students too were smooth and gleaming. May, the Asian girl (Chinese as it turned out), had thick shiny hair. David, the American boy, had a freshly ironed shirt neatly tucked into his trousers, and Ella and Lauren, the Canadian girls, smiled with straight white teeth. They spoke of their travels, the weather and each other's cities in slow polite voices:

'We've done Thailand, Malaysia, Vietnam, *so pretty*, Indonesia, Bali, *awesome*, and soon we're going to South America . . .'

I had barely recognised them when I entered the breakfast hall, as if their faces had been wiped clean overnight along with the plates, eyes and lips scrubbed clean of honey stains and breadcrumbs.

May and I spoke a little after the others had gone out shopping. Her handshake was soggy and her skin felt smooth like the peanut butter on the white bread in front of me. She had served herself a huge plate of Coco Pops, a large mug of hot chocolate, a glass of milk and some bread.

'European food,' she said and smiled, while she used a spoon to scoop out a massive wad of butter from the butter dish, spreading it unevenly on the slice of bread. 'I love milk,' she continued. I smiled back at her and put my knife in a jar of peanut butter.

'You like . . .' May struggled to find the right word. '. . . Club?'

'Club?'

'Dancing . . .' She slurped her cocoa.

'Ah, nightclub,' I said. 'I don't go out much.'

'OK, yes. I like.'

'Really? Do you go out much at home?'

'Yes, me and friends. Dancing, singing . . .' May tried to squeeze her spoon into a small pack of jam where it wouldn't fit.

'It's easier with a knife,' I said.

'Oh,' she said and blushed.

The university had left big envelopes in the reception, containing welcome letters, a map of the campus and information about the different trips and social events in and outside of Aybourne. The events had funny titles: 'You Talkin' to Me?' was a class in conversational English, and 'Fish'n'Chippin' Aybourne' was a fishing trip. The first event was called 'Tackle the Town'. I hadn't got round to checking what it was yet, but the other students at the hostel seemed so excited that I came with them. Alice, an American lady from the foreign exchange office, picked us up, and we got the tram down to a huge stadium where we watched a rugby match between two local teams. Alice showed us to our seats and said informative things like *Here you see the Aybourne Dragons' supporters with their green and white scarves, and of course an Aybrew ale, that's our local beer*. The students all went to the kiosk, where we bought our own Aybrews and little pies. My pie lay in my hand, lukewarm and dense. It looked like an inflated yellow beer cap.

'What's in the pie?' I asked Lauren, one of the Canadian girls.

'Kidney and brown sauce,' she replied. I deposited the little kidney gently on an empty seat. Then we went back to our places and tried to find out which team was winning.

'This is not like ice-hockey,' giggled Lauren. She pointed out towards the pitch. 'Look at those tiny shorts! They're almost naked, *yummy!*'

Next to me, May smiled. I thought of the man on the tram, and wanted to tell her about him, but didn't know what word to use. *Penis, dick, cock?* On the pitch men were throwing themselves at other men, and Alice waved her arms, yelling things like *And here you see a maul . . . a maul is . . .* Every time someone got a knee to the crotch or a foot to the chest, a shudder went through the audience, and I could feel that same shudder go through my own body, feel it lifting us for a moment before we slowly sank back into our seats.

After the match, empty Aybrew bottles and napkins, sweet wrappers and plates were left lying on the benches and on the street outside. In the town centre the shops were closed and the restaurants empty. The student group split. Alice got a tram to the beach, Ella and Lauren went to a pub, May went to meet the Chinese student society, and I walked slowly back to the hostel alone, headphones on. I felt a need for something familiar in the strange, dark streets, something from Norway, so I put on Kings of Convenience. They sang in harmony, one voice for each of the tram tracks that gleamed in the dark next to me. They sang slowly as I was closing in on the hostel by the pier.

Later I felt the walls of the attic close in, collapse around me and shut out the world. The music separated me from the sound of cars, wind, and my own steps.

In the middle of the night I heard May on the phone in the hallway. The sounds of her alien language bubbled, as if they came out of and into her mouth at the same time. Half asleep, I pictured the words as lines of knives and spoons. After she hung up, I heard her feet shuffle into her bathroom. There she pulled down her trousers and sat on the toilet seat. Urine streamed against the porcelain bowl. In the darkness I thought it sounded a little thick, as if warm milk was trickling out of her.

The Chest

THE NEXT DAY the weather had cleared and as I didn't want to attend 'You Talkin' to Me?' with the others, I decided to walk around Aybourne alone instead. I wandered along the tram tracks between whitewashed buildings and posters advertising cars, diet yoghurts and energy drinks. The sea followed me on the far side. Islands that I could barely see the day before gleamed in the sunshine.

First I tried to reach the edge of town, but no matter what direction I walked I was forced to turn back. The last stop on one of the tracks ended at an orbital motorway that ran parallel to an electric sheep fence, and I could go no further. In the other direction I found a golf course that ran from the last of the town streets all the way down to the beach. Between the town and the golf course the broad South Gate motorway ran, and I couldn't find a way to cross it. Eventually I walked upwards to the hills, towards the mountains. This route ended in a picnic area and some dustbins. After that there was nothing. Aybourne was beneath me, closed off in all directions, like a chest with no lid.

Next, I tried to find the university. When I got back into the town centre I pulled out the torn map I'd found in the dining room at the hostel. The map stained my fingers, as if it were melting. My fingertips were decorated with imprints of roads and parks. After a little while I had lost my way completely, and I was unsure whether the map I had was old or even if it was for the right town.

The third time I thought I'd found the campus, I realised that I was the one at fault, not the map. I wasn't on university grounds but I had entered an overgrown garden. It lay by a gigantic grey brick building with archways at the entrance and a pointy Victorian clock tower at the top. This must be city hall, I thought, my finger still on the map, because that was supposed to be in front of the campus. And when I looked closely I could see a faded old engraving on the dark wall: *City Hall.* A narrow path twisted through the garden towards the archways and when I followed it I found an old sundial in the tall grass. It was around a metre tall, like a pulpit, and wrought in iron with ornaments around its foot. I bent over the sundial to see if it showed the time, but the long dark shadow from the clock tower fell across it, and the sundial was rendered useless, a face without features.

In between the archways someone waved at me, and I noticed the Canadian girls. I waved back and walked over to them.

'We're going for dinner, do you wanna join us?' asked Lauren.

I nodded, happy not to be alone.

In the café I again ordered the dish that was easiest to pronounce.

'Your English is really great,' Lauren said.

'Better than ours!' They laughed, and she continued: 'Have you ever lived in England?'

'No, but we're taught it in school a lot.'

Lauren and Ella kept chatting about the night before, with big chunks of hamburger in their mouths. They spoke fast about excursions they were going on and said that the university had too little focus on sports and that the town was too windy.

'Have you found a place to live yet?' Ella asked.

'No.'

'We're seeing some places tomorrow. If you like you can borrow our newspaper,' she said and handed me the classified section, dappled with coffee stains and crossings-out.

All the students at the hostel were trying to find permanent accommodation. I spent the next three days in and out of phone boxes, scheduling meetings and visiting numerous flat shares. Mostly they were in apartment blocks, or big two-floored terraces further from the town centre. They were home to neurotic students or hippies with marijuana plants in the back garden. I ran into the Canadians again and again in different apartments. They were confident and tanned and made the tenants laugh. Next to them I felt sombre and pale – *The serious Norwegian*, Lauren joked. I walked like a ghost through the rooms in house after house, while the visits weaved together in my head, becoming an endless braid of faces, corridors, and small, unfurnished rooms with plaster rosettes around the ceiling lights.

A group of art students who lived in one of the big terrace houses decided to turn their open day into a party. On the balcony a boy with bushy hair and a leather jacket read beat poetry, another served lukewarm punch, and downstairs in the kitchen a girl played guitar and sang Ani DiFranco in a shaky voice. She was wearing a bandana and her legs were unshaven.

'Are you vegan?' she asked after she had stopped singing. I shook my head.

'It doesn't matter if you're not. But you should try.'

I nodded. The girl with the bandana shrugged and began a new song.

In between my interviews I sat on park benches and waited for time to pass, alongside homeless people drinking cider from cheap two-litre bottles. They didn't ask why I didn't have furniture or how old I was or why my English was so good.

'You're young, aren't you,' said an older lady sat next to me. That was all. She opened a can of raspberry vodka and didn't look at me again. Her mascara was running down her cheeks.

The viewings continued. In house after house I left my name and the hostel's phone number, like a dog marking lampposts. Most people said they would ring when they had come to a decision. In my notebook I jotted down names and addresses, for reference when they called. But no one did, and after searching non-stop for four days I was still without a place to live. On the way home, I caught a tram and passed several stops before I realised it was going in the wrong direction. I got off on a deserted main road and had started the walk back when I heard a deep voice shout from a passing car:

NICE TITS, BITCH!

And then he drove off, fast, and the 'TCH drowned in the noise of the engine. I could feel my cheeks burn and I pulled my jacket tighter around myself.

When I finally got back to the hostel I was tired, cold and certain I didn't want to talk to anyone, but the receptionist stopped me in the doorway:

'Someone called for you and left this message.'

She handed me a yellow, folded note. I thanked her and unfolded the paper, excited to see whether I'd been offered a room, but it was just a friendly rejection from the bandana girl:

> Dear Jo, the room in 21 Primrose St
> is now taken. We chose two
> Canadian girls. Thanks for coming.

The Shadows

THIS IS HOW I remember my first day at the university: my shadow slipped between big stone stairs, benches and fountains. Groups of students who already knew each other were everywhere. They talked loud and fast and showed each other books and schedules. Among these sounds, my booted steps were inaudible.

On campus the tall brick buildings shut out the rest of town. Some had spires that looked like the City Hall clock tower. On a large lawn outside the library the student societies had put up tables and colourful banners. *Join the Christian Student Organisation,* one of them said in cramped handwriting. *University of Aybourne Queer Society* was painted on another in vivid rainbow colours.

'It's No Diet Day,' a girl shouted after me outside the main building of the biology institute, Earth

Sciences. She had dreadlocks and a rainbow-patterned T-shirt.

'I'm sorry?'

'*No Diet Day*,' she repeated. 'Today we celebrate the fat!' She then handed me a sweaty chocolate muffin from a plastic tray. 'No Diet Day,' I repeated to myself. I continued to replay snippets of conversations that I overheard around me while I walked to the Earth Sciences department and until I got to the lecture hall door.

The hall was a huge auditorium, filled with students. I walked between the benches looking for an empty seat. The rows slanted steeply towards the lectern at the bottom, and on the second row from the front someone finally scooted over to offer me a seat. Behind me I could hear the rustle of paper: hundreds of students leafing through information sheets from folders titled *New Bachelor of Science Students – Welcome Session*. One of the professors was then introduced, and he started to tell us about the university regulations, about the bachelor's degree and about biology studies. I jotted down new magical words in my notebook: *tutorial, prerequisite, curriculum, research thesis.* Then I noted some academic terms: *cell theory, homoeostasis, endothermic.* I silently mouthed the new words, and hung on every term I recognised and almost recognised.

———

During the induction day I became increasingly aware how unprepared I was to study in English. After the welcome session we were divided into small groups and asked to introduce ourselves. While I waited my turn I noticed how all the students' voices went up on the last syllable in every sentence. Everything they said sounded like a question: *My name is Alistair?* Or *I'm Catrìona? From Aybourne South?* It sounded like they didn't know their names or where they lived. When it was my turn, my voice was stiff and rusty. In short spurts I told them my name and where I was from, but every pause was too long and the syllables too short. The language grated on my throat. The words were wrong: *Norway* was not a country I'd been to, and it felt like a lie to pronounce my name as *Djåoanna*. And even before Johanna, when I said, *Hello, my name is*, I couldn't help but think of other names, from pop songs and films: *My name is Luka*, I sang to myself, *My name is Jonas*, gurgled behind my tongue when I said, 'Djåoanna, Djåo.' When I finished, I was almost certain that I had said something else, a different name, some-thing wrong. I suddenly knew nothing about myself, nothing seemed right in English, nothing was true.

There was only one first-year at the Faculty of Science who wasn't from the area. She was German, and when she introduced herself as *Fran-ziska-from-Ham-burg*, I recognised my own stiff delivery at once. Her voice had a depth that made it more confident than mine. It sounded calm and shockingly serious in comparison with the light question-inflections coming from the other students. Franziska and I walked out together after the seminar. We were both a couple of years older than most of the students, and she seemed happy to meet someone else who wasn't a native.

'Where do you live?' I asked.

'I live down on South Beach, with my brother. He's been living here for a couple of years, so I was lucky. Where do you live?'

'I'm looking.'

'Did you see many places?'

'Yes, no one wants me yet though.'

'Most people probably want someone they know, or someone who can't just run off. You know, back to another country. That's what my brother says anyway. But there's a place on campus with listings. I can show you before I go.'

It was late in the day. Most of the students had gone home. The listings were hanging in the window of a café at the far end of the campus. Lots of handwritten notes formed a city map of index cards, showing the way to abandoned apartments, dusty bedrooms and old cars. Some included colourful drawings of cute cats or lively explanations for why a new tenant was needed. 'Are you our dancing queen?' it said on a note stuck in the middle, and another one read, 'Desperately seeking YOU! (If you love cats.)'

One note stuck out, on the edge of the clump. It had no drawings, puns or patterns:

ROOM AVAILABLE IN LARGE W.HOUSE.
SHARE WITH 1 F.
.QUIET.

There followed an address and a phone number. The word QUIET, closed in by a full stop on either side, had an emphasis I liked. Quiet worked for me. I couldn't imagine the other girl, only large rooms, unfurnished and uninhabited. And when I rang from the phone box by City Hall, the girl didn't have a voice either, only a mechanical one from the phone company:

You have reached the answering machine of ... Car-ral ... John-ston. Please leave a message after the tone, or hang up.

While I listened to the mechanical voice, I saw a boy step through the City Hall garden, pass the sundial and head towards the phone box I was in. He was extremely skinny and an oversized windbreaker hung loose around his upper body. I stepped out of the phone box and started to walk down the street when I saw him turn towards me. He looked at me for a moment before he lifted his hands and put his index finger in a hole he had made with the fingers on his other hand.

'How much?' he asked while he continued to move the finger in and out of the hole. I felt myself become hot and cold at the same time, turned and started to walk the other way while I heard the boy laugh behind me. Then I heard another sound: the sound of someone retching. When I turned around the corner I saw him heaving into a bin. Afterwards he walked to a bench and sat there, calm and smiling, while he wiped his mouth.

I picture my own body that afternoon, between the archways along City Hall. I imagine, more and more people between me and the boy, more and more houses that become more and more blocks, more and more songs on my Minidisc player. It doesn't help: inside me the boy continues to put his index finger through his hand, slowly but firmly, as if he is poking it inside my body, and then he retches again. I can't get rid of the finger, the sound, the image. It's as if I'm the throat that makes him vomit. Long after I've returned to the hostel, I still see him behind my eyelids, stood by City Hall and becoming smaller and smaller, throwing up again and again.

The Apartment

THE HAWTHORN DISTRICT, with its old factories, was situated a little outside the town, beneath the mountains in the east. I'd seen the buildings on my walks, and they would look back at me with their grimy square windows. In the daytime the area seemed uninhabited and frozen, silent as a photograph, but when I stepped off the tram I could hear music and see light and shadow move behind the windowpanes. Behind me the tram wheels screeched against the tracks, the wheels howling as it headed for the next stop. I turned off onto a road surrounded by red-brick houses. The road led to a huge old silo complex with eight cylindrical towers that reached up to the sky like a set of massive organ pipes. I noticed a little alley among the brick houses. That was where I was going.

The alley was unlit, and the old asphalt was full of cracks. Wet weeds were bent and then crushed beneath my shoes. I stopped in front of a big square warehouse with a flickering shimmer coming from a small window up by the roof. The rest of the wall was dark and smooth. When I knocked, the whole house was still black water beneath my hand.

The knocking seemed unnaturally loud. The echoes unrolled slowly, in and out of the sound of the tram tracks and of a car's engine at a nearby multistorey car park. Then it was quiet. No footsteps or voices sounded from inside. I knocked once more, a little firmer. This time a light started flickering in the window under the roof, but still no sound. Maybe Carral Johnston thought it was too late for visitors, or perhaps she'd found a tenant already. I was about to start planning my route back to the hostel when the door opened.

The old warehouse interior had been renovated into an apartment with thin dividing walls made from plaster-board that didn't quite reach halfway to the ceiling. The spaces behind them seemed more like booths than rooms. Carral Johnston gave me a tour of the plaster-board labyrinth. She was a slender girl, a few years older than me, wearing a tight pastel-yellow wool jumper that almost matched her pale yellow-white skin. Her yellow curls were tied up in a ponytail that rocked back and forth over her shoulders while she walked over the wooden floors with long silent steps. My boots thumped after her. Inside, too, I seemed to make unnaturally loud noises that buzzed on the tin ceiling above us.

We wound up by the kitchen table in the middle of the building, where the yellow Carral Johnston sat with her legs up on a chair. While she told me a little about herself – that she was from Brighton, that she had been here for three years, and that she worked as an office temp – I sat and watched her feet through the steam from my tea. Her toes curled up over a small fan heater, and her arched ankles made the movement look like a ballet exercise. In my boots my own feet were arching, as if they were trying to copy her movement.

'So, Jo, what do you think?' she asked smiling and continued without waiting for my reply: 'We have a washing machine, TV, mattresses, everything we need. Plus a whole lot of *weirdness*. It's an old warehouse after all. When I first moved in, I thought it was a little scary.'

I nodded and wondered whether I was part of this 'we', even though I had never been to her apartment before.

'But it's not scary, just different,' she continued and leant towards me. 'The house has a life of its own. You get used to it. Excuse me for a moment.'

Carral put her arched feet back on the floor, stood up and walked to the bathroom. When she left my sight, it was as if something took over the house, and it seemed to rock. The floor panels were rubbing against each other, the plasterboard swaycd like long blades of grass. The thermostat clicked on and off, unable to decide whether the room was warm enough or not. The world outside rattled against the window. From the bathroom I could hear the sound of denim pulled over skin, the sound of skin coming to rest on porcelain, and finally a trickling, increasing and eventually steady stream of water.

'Sound travels here.'

Her voice, bathed in echo, came from everywhere, as if she was speaking from the floorboards, the fan heater, the kitchen clock. The stream continued.

'Luckily I'm pretty quiet.'

Only a small drip was to be heard now, a pause, and then finally crumpled tissue being dragged against skin.

'Paper-thin walls,' Carral said and giggled, but the sound of flushing drowned her laughter. 'As I said, that's just what this place is like.' She opened the door again, returned to her chair and put her feet up on the heater. The tea had stopped steaming. She put her hands around the mug with a satisfied smile, as if she had accomplished something.

I hadn't met a lot of girls who talked while they peed, and definitely not a lot of girls who talked *about* peeing while they did it. There's usually a lull in the conversation even when you're sat in neighbouring cubicles. Maybe peeing and talking is a bit like singing and playing an instrument at the same time, I thought, two sets of muscles having to work side by side.

'Your English is great by the way,' she said and smiled.

'Oh,' I said, 'we all grow up with the BBC where I'm from.'

'Well, I've met other Norwegians. They all had terrible American accents.' She still smiled the same interested smile.

'You're probably right,' I said.

'Speaking of you . . . Why did you come to Aybourne?'

'I'm studying biology. Bachelor of Science, I think it's called.'

'But here? Why would you study here?'

'I wanted to come here,' I answered. 'It's a good university.'

'So you've left everything behind to live here for three years. I hope you don't have a boyfriend waiting for you back in Norway.'

Carral giggled teasingly and put her arms behind her head. The thin jumper pulled over her belly and the fabric tightened over her breasts. I couldn't see any trace of her nipples.

'No boyfriend,' I replied in the calmest tone I could muster.

'Sounds good. You're so young.'

Later that evening, after I had checked out of the hostel and said goodbye to the wank mirror and the golf clubs wrapped in black body bags behind the reception desk,

I lay awake in my new bed and listened to Carral leaf through the pages of a book. I heard her fingers scrape the rough paper, the spine creak and the binding tighten. Later when I woke up my light was out but I could make out a glimmering halo of light over her bedroom wall, and in almost imperceptible noises at night I imagined hearing the hint of her curls falling over her cheek as she turned. Later the fridge started to hum. I was sure I heard tiny ripples on the surface of the milk inside its carton.

The Apples

WITH ITS OPEN SPACES, ladders and plasterboard walls, the factory is little more than the skeleton of an apartment. The ceiling – which makes for a silver-grey, gloomy sky – is several metres high. By the kitchen table in the middle of the cube, an iron post runs like a spine from floor to ceiling. Under the ceiling, thick old beams are coated in silverfish and dust. On three of the room's sides, mezzanines have been built, half-way up each wall. Two of these are small decks framed by particle board walls. They face each other on the north and south sides. On the east wall is an open mezzanine with a railing. It's big enough to serve as a living room and contains a television, a sofa, and pillows on the floor. A staircase leads here from the kitchen. Carral stores old things under the mezzanine: stiff sheets, a dishwasher, tinned food and old broken wooden chairs. The bathroom is in the west and has a toilet and bathtub, fenced by the same thin particle board walls as the mezzanines. The boards reach just over our heads and next to the bathroom is a ladder that leads up to a small balcony on the roof of the apartment next door.

A mattress in the northern mezzanine, next to the bathroom, is my bed. Across from me, above the entrance, is the mezzanine where Carral sleeps, and under it hangs an old chandelier that jingles when she turns in bed. Standing on the raised platform of my bedroom I can see above the boards and down into the kitchen, across to the open mezzanine and, if I stretch, right down to the toilet seat in the bathroom.

'Do you know what kind of factory this used to be?' I asked while I tossed my clothes onto the mezzanine. On the wall above the loft I'd seen big square pieces of metal and imagined they once had huge hooks or wax candles hanging from them. But Carral didn't reply, and when I came downstairs to get some more clothes from the box on the floor, I saw that she was sat by the kitchen table with a thick book.

'Did you say something?' she asked.

'I was just wondering what they used to make here.'

'I'm not sure, but it's been a while since there's been any kind of industry in this area.'

I nodded and Carral continued:

'I wonder a lot about what they were thinking when they converted the place.'

'It doesn't seem quite finished.'

'Not finished? I think it looks like a theatre set. I mean, like, plasterboard in the bathroom.' She laughed and went back to her book.

'What are you reading?' I asked.

'Oh, just a romance. Kind of stupid. I studied literature a few years ago, and now I only read trash. I'm a hypocrite! Do you need help, by the way?'

'No, you just read.'

I went back to my pile of clothes. Carral kept reading. Sometimes she looked up to dunk her biscuit in a tea-cup, and from my mezzanine I could hear her suck tea from the biscuit and turn the page at regular intervals.

The house was raw and porous. It didn't shut out the world outside like the houses at home, and there was no paint or wallpaper anywhere, just naked boards and rough concrete walls. In the bathroom the walls were soft and damp. Dark mould spotted the corners. Norwegian houses, I explained to Carral, are hermetic, warm wooden tanks filled with colour, and Norwegian sounds are kept discrete by dry, well-insulated walls. In the factory, on the other hand, I only truly felt like I was inside when I slept and slumber put up its heavy impenetrable walls between the conscious world and me. Monday morning I woke very early to the clanking of bottles as the first drunks returned from the Aygros Supermarket around the corner. I stayed in bed and listened to the increasing rush: cars that drove up and up the spiralling ramp in the multistorey a few streets away; sidewalks being hosed down and swept; the trams hooting along on the main road. Maybe it wasn't the house, but me that was porous, I thought. Maybe I had to grow a thicker skin in this town.

In the living room on the open deck I sat down by the only exterior window. It was still early and up here I could look at the people and the fog and sometimes feel the morning sun on my face. Everywhere else there was just pale light from naked bulbs hanging from the ceiling on long wires. Like seismometers, they swayed at any movement in the house. Not even the big chandelier hanging under Carral's bed gave much light. It didn't do much more than reflect the sunlight from the window in its glass splinters and cast a dim glow of light on the kitchen floor. A fine shower of dust drifted to the floor when Carral stood up on the mezzanine.

In the dim light, my hearing became more acute. The open factory brimmed with echoes. Waves of sound could persist and resonate between the walls, filling out the silence until other noises took over. When Carral zipped up her jacket and tied her shoelaces that morning, I could hear faint traces of her earlier activity:

vague sonic contours of shower and toothbrush, yawning and chewing. When she left for the big Sachs & Sachs building where she worked, the shattering sound of the front door shutting was thousands of tiny marbles rolling through the house. I turned to the window to see her walk to the tram stop. There was no one else on the road. The broken windows of the building abutting the silos glittered in the sun.

I hadn't started on my reading list yet. There was no reason to delay. The semester began in earnest in a few days and I was tired of walking the streets. On the first page of the biology compendium it said in bold letters

> All natural objects belong to one of two primary categories: The non-living and the living. What we call biology is the study of the living.

I liked what I read – *the study of the living* – and when I went downstairs to make tea, I noticed the living all around the house: a small white spider crawled on the windowsill, the boards bulged as if beetles and larvae were crawling inside them, and in the kettle on the kitchen counter the water had begun to bubble, a sign that I was among the living. While I considered whether I should put milk and sugar in my tea like a Brit, I repeated the words out loud: *What we call biology is the study of the living,* and after I had said it, it was almost as if I heard the words continue to move between the concrete walls, as if I stood in the wild between two cliffs listening to the echo. Did the beetles, the larvae, and the spiders hear it?

When Carral came back and I looked up from my compendium, I was surprised to find it was already evening. Outside the window the sun had set, and the city's contours were sketched out in electric light with the sea behind it like a black mouth. I climbed down to Carral from the living room as she arched her back and lifted a white carrier bag to the kitchen table.

'Look what I got!' she said, and from the top of the bag a whole pile of apples rolled out onto the kitchen table: coloured pink, burgundy red and gold. 'They were being thrown out.'

Together we put some in a fruit bowl and the rest in the fridge. Carral was clearly thinking that we would eat them all. 'They just, like, lay there,' she said. 'Do you like apples?'

I nodded. I liked the sound of Carral's mouth as she took a huge bite out of one of the golden apples and crushed the sweet flesh between her teeth. The soft yellow of the peel was almost the same as her hair.

'They have pretty names,' she continued. 'I saw in the shop. The pink ones are called Pink Ladies, and the yellow Honeygolds. Isn't that nice?'

'Very. What about the red ones, what are they called?'

'That's the best one. Bloody Ploughman.'

'Wow,' I said.

Carral held up a red apple.

'They look like the apples mum used to hang on the Christmas tree,' she said.

'Real apples?'

'No, they were wooden, painted red. They looked so nice that I tried to eat them.'

'Oh no!'

'Oh yeah! I lost a tooth.' She wiped her mouth and continued: 'The day after I got an apple for pudding, a toffee apple, you know. Even though my mouth was really sore.'

'Could you eat it?'

'I licked it.'

Carral took another bite of her Honeygold apple. Her teeth met resistance in the flesh, and I heard them push further in.

'There's a worm that eats apple cores, and sometimes drowns in fruit juice,' I said while I crumpled up the empty apple bag. A whiff of apple rose from the bag and spread through the room, and I imagined that the smell seeped into the concrete walls and boards, into the kitchen chairs and the cutting board.

'So far I'm good,' she answered and smirked with apple juice bubbling between her teeth.

When she chewed I could hear the sound of the fruit's flesh dissolving into foam.

I didn't know then that the hiss and bubble from her mouth would soon be heard in other places, in ways I didn't yet understand. An apple is never just an apple. Carral peeled a Honeygold, and long round coils of peel curled and fell on the kitchen table. I took a bite of a Bloody Ploughman. Even the flesh was red.

'Bloody,' Carral said.

'Nice colour,' I answered.

'It looks sinful. I bet that was the apple Eve ate, you know, in the Bible, the forbidden fruit.'

'Might be. But I've eaten some too now. Does that mean you have to kick me out of your house?'

I held the half-eaten apple out to her. She burst out laughing and pointed out at the factory: 'Does this look like Paradise or what?'

It was evening. Carral chitchatted and leafed through a glossy magazine while chewing on her thumb nail. The apples rubbed gently against each other in the cupboard and in the bowl. The glass shards in the chandelier clinked. In my biology compendium I read a chapter on extinct sea creatures. The TV was muted and flickered behind my back, reflected on the railing. And all the while I could hear this hiss and bubble that I still didn't understand, as if we were far down on a quiet seabed and listening to wind howling on the surface.

When Carral went to bed, I heard fabric against skin and fabric against fabric as she undressed behind the wall on her mezzanine. She'd left her thick book on the kitchen table. It had a faint fruity smell.

'Good night,' I said.

And night came and went. Next morning it was raining, and I woke up to the drumbeat of raindrops on the roof, the pattering noise never quite keeping a rhythm. Through the drumming something else could be heard: apple skin against wood, rolling through the kitchen, back and forth, like eggs ready to hatch.

The Fruitpearls

A WEEK CAME AND WENT. I walked through the wide white aisles of the Aygros Supermarket, buying yoghurt, cheese and milk that looked nothing like the yoghurt, cheese and milk from home. Everything was fattier, sweeter, saltier, bigger. At university I filled my schedule with Biology of Cells and Organisms and Genetics and The Evolution of Life. In my first lecture I learned that millions of years ago Aybourne and most of the surrounding landmass had been below water. The professor explained how the ground had been covered by a thick layer of limestone formed by billions of tiny little algae skeletons.

'Think about it,' he continued eagerly, 'if the water was still here, only a few church spires and the City Hall clock tower would reach above the surface.'

Afternoons I spent with Franziska on the lawn outside
Earth Sciences.

'Are you enjoying your factory?'

'Yeah, I like it,' I answered.

'It seems really strange. You said there are no walls?'

I picked at the sugar on my napkin from a cinnamon
doughnut. The sugar crystals stuck to my fingertip.

'Only thin plasterboard. It's weird, but it's ok.' I put
my finger in my mouth and crushed the sugar between
my teeth.

'I don't think I could live like that.'

'Me neither, really,' I answered.

But I did live in this factory, and I'd started to like it.
I enjoyed listening to Carral's sounds, how she shuffled
across the kitchen floor or dried off with a towel after
she'd showered. From my bed I could hear her pee at
night, a faint, muted trickling against the toilet bowl,
which made me imagine, half-asleep, thin flowing
golden ribbons.

Gradually I got used to listening to the factory and
Carral and the whole district, and one morning I didn't
wake up when the Aygros Supermarket opened. I no
longer heard the cars in the car park at night. And in a
similar way I grew accustomed to all of Aybourne, and
I no longer missed the taste of brown bread and liver
paste, and I poured the right amount of milk in my tea
without thinking about how I didn't used to drink tea
with milk back in Norway. When I walked towards the

kitchen table and sat down with my milky tea, the floor-boards creaked just as they did in response to Carral's pattering feet.

The apples spread all over the flat. Half-rotten fruit was left in the bin, on dirty plates and in used coffee mugs. Some apples were left forgotten on the bigger mezzanine, others rolled into corners and under cupboards. Every morning while tying up her shoelaces and buttoning her jacket, Carral put an apple for lunch on the chest of drawers by the front door. Every morning she forgot it. Every evening she took a bite of an apple as she came home, and left it on the kitchen table or the bench. Sometimes I sat and watched the apple; how the juices dribbled from the bite marks. I wondered what was apple juice and what was her spit, and thought about licking the place where she'd bit to see if I could tell the difference. But I didn't. I continued to study it, watching the flesh turn yellow and then brown.

After a week the remaining apples had turned soft, and we stopped eating them. Instead I used my finger-nails to make patterns in the skin of a Honeygold while I read *Introductory Mycology*:

> But what are fungi? Traditionally, biologists have defined fungi as eukaryote, organisms that produce spores and that reproduce sexually and asexually.

When I looked up from the book, I saw that I'd made a little circle-shaped nail mark in the middle of the yellow apple. The edges had already dried up, and the tear was brown, a small dark nipple in the golden skin. My fingers smelled of yeast.

When I returned home from that week's last lecture, I found Carral and a pile of apples on the floor. She had tried to collect them and put them back in the bag, but the bag had torn and the apples were rolling everywhere.

'They stink,' she said, picking up a Pink Lady apple and squeezing it until the skin burst. The fermented pulp oozed over her hand. She dropped the apple and shook her fingers. Muscles tensed in her arm and in her neck under her yellow curls.

'They're just a little old,' I said.

'They're not *that* old,' she replied and picked up a new carrier bag from the drawer. 'And they're rotten already.'

'They were old when you got them. All fruit rots when it gets old.'

'Sure,' she said.

I walked towards her and picked up the apple she had dropped. It was yellow-brown and shiny around the tear in the peel. 'It's when they tear that they go mouldy,' I explained to Carral and pointed to the tear. 'Look.'

'Just throw it out,' she said. 'Some previous tenant left a composter outside.'

'I'll take them.'

She held the bag while I put the apples in it, yellow-brown and red, soft and wet. I got them from the cupboards, the mezzanine and from the kitchen bench, I picked up the apples that had fallen to the floor and rolled along the floorboards. A sticky dark-red Bloody Ploughman got stuck to my hand, and I thought about Carral's comment about Eve and the forbidden fruit; imagining I was cleaning up after the Fall.

In the compost outside the apples looked like jewels in a jewellery box. I closed the container carefully and sat on the lid. Carral smoked a cigarette on the stair. She smiled groggily.

'Sorry I got stressed out. I don't like rotten things.'

I looked down on the compost lid underneath me, as if to make sure the apples stayed there.

'It's been a while since I lived with someone.'

'Is it weird to share again?'

'It's fine, it's just kind of new. The apartment feels . . . different.'

'Smaller, perhaps?'

'Maybe. Or just unfamiliar.'

'It gets crowded quickly,' I said. 'With all those apples.'

She laughed and put the cigarette out under her shoe.

We leave the front door open. The fermented smell disappears over the doorstep, mixes with rain and wind and the tram's whining progress. All that's left is the trail of brown juice on the bench and seeds between the floorboards. But my dreams are full of apples, and in the dark my body slowly transforms into fruit: tonsils shrinking to seeds and lungs to cores. I dream of white flowers blossoming under my nails, as if under ice. Then my nails break, opening up like clams and in the finger flesh there are little sticky fruit pearls.

The Double Sleep

THE SIGHT OF HER startled me. I couldn't quite believe she had been sitting in the same room for half an hour without me realising. It looked like she was sleeping, but maybe she'd been sitting there with her eyes closed, listening to the sounds I make only when I'm alone: the sound of my fingers scratching thick pubic hair, lips slipping apart in small sighs, the elastic in my underpants snapping against my skin as my hand slides free. Carral sat on the mezzanine stairs, only a couple of metres away. She supported her head gently on the railing, silent as furniture. Eyes closed, lips pushed together. Not a muscle moved. Not a joint clicked. I quickly closed my flies while I looked at her. Her head kept nodding. Her collarbone protruded each time.

Carral's bobbing head didn't break her sleep. It was as if she dreamt of sleeping and being awoken, trapped in a double sleep. I finished reading the chapter in my biology compendium, mostly so she wouldn't think she'd scared me, and afterwards I went downstairs to the kitchen and started preparing vegetables on the counter. At first I moved quietly so as not to wake her, moving crabwise between the fridge and the stove, dicing and peeling slowly and silently. But then I grew tired of her weird sleeping and began to make more noise. I turned on the radio, chopped onions and potatoes hard and fast, frying them up in the pan. Still no sound came from the stairs. Why didn't she wake up? Was she trying to get to me, make me self-conscious? At this thought, I made an effort to be even louder. But it wasn't until I'd served the food, put the kettle on – Carral long since given up on – that I heard anything from her. A long yawn sounded through the metal pipes in the railings, a finger joint clicked, a cotton sweater stretched, feet shuffled down the stairs. When I turned around, she was gone.

A little later she came and sat by the kitchen table. I was eating.

'Did you fall asleep on the mezzanine today?' I asked.

'I guess I did,' she said. 'Sometimes I don't sleep too well at night.'

She was wearing that thin pale-yellow wool sweater again. The yellow was so close to her skin tone and hair that she seemed naked, a sexless, matted nakedness. I cut the yolk from my fried egg and put it in my mouth. The yolk burst under my tongue, and I imagined it was her skin I was tasting, but she didn't move, just continued to twirl a finger in her ponytail, looking down at the novel opened in front of her. I licked the sticky yellow from my teeth.

'Have you been home long?'

'All afternoon. Didn't you hear me before?'

'You were home? No, I didn't hear,' she said slowly, without looking up.

But I could hear her every move as the night settled in, and when we sat on the mezzanine again, I stared at her yellow sweater, trying to see a hint of nipple under the tight-knit wool fabric. There was nothing. Above us the light bulbs swung back and forth, like little golden eggs.

The Moonlip

IN THE COMING DAYS I brought more and more things to the apartment: library books and pens, clothes and pillows, tea bags and tinned beans. At the same time the wind was picking up in Aybourne; it dragged seaweed clusters and sand into the town centre, moved benches along the beach walk and bent grass and autumn flowers in the university's botanical garden to a smooth fur. When I staggered to the tram stop, the silo pipes behind me howled. Shattered windows glared out over the street like the gigantic closed eyes of a sphinx.

The wind doubled my commute into town, and when I finally reached the Earth Sciences building the door to the lecture hall was closed. On the door was a small noticeboard where an old drawing was pinned, a caricature of a professor with thick bushy hair chasing a group of small, terrified students. Below the drawing it said in printed letters:

> The world of the living is a hierarchy, where each level in the biological chain feeds off of the level below.

I carefully opened the door and snuck into the auditorium.

Today's lecture was about reproduction. Dr Spencer Lipman, whose nickname was Spitlip, enunciated every word slowly and clearly, and every time his lips contracted and split apart again to make a *p* or a *b*, he shot tiny spit pearls from his mouth. After a while white froth formed at the corner of his lips. I wiped my own mouth and had to look away, forced to look down in the notebook in front of me. In it I had just written,

> Fungi have varied methods of reproduction. They produce and spread huge amounts of spores. When conditions are right, the population can double in a very short time.

I couldn't help but think about the spit-bubbles on Lipman's mouth, this population of tiny drops spreading like little wet seeds across the auditorium. On my hand a little watery bead blinked.

The same night I found Carral sleeping on the sofa again, silent and soft, barely breathing. She was in the same position as yesterday. Her neck had sunk into her shoulders, her whole body seemed to have collapsed into itself, her head bobbing loosely on top. Her hair lay curled along the banister. Some of her locks twirled around the railings. Outside, the streets glistened with rain, and further off the last remnants of dusk were tipped into the sea, or maybe they were just clouds.

The novel I'd seen her read lay open next to one of her sleeping hands. I bent over Carral and studied her face: it was tender and still, not an eyelid moved. When I had reassured myself she was asleep, I took the book. On the back there was a library stamp, and on the inside of the cover was a little envelope with a library card inside. A sticky stain ran along the fore edge. On the front, one side of the cover was torn, while the other showed a pair of full lips, a pack of wolves with their snouts in the air, and a huge, shining full moon at the top of the picture. The title was positioned between the wolves and the moon in slanted script: *Moon Lips*.

I leafed through the pages: title page, copyright, contents . . . The introduction began,

This isn't just any romance in your hands, dear reader . . .

And then the first chapter:

> Miranda Darling's lips were full and succulent, the
> envy of her friends and torment of her frustrated suit-
> ors. By day, you might think her mouth like a cherry,
> and by night, when she graced the balcony to sip a tall
> glass of Campari, the gloss on her lips rivalled the
> moonlight.

I turned the pages for a little while. *Moon Lips* seemed
to be typical pulp. I wasn't very interested in Miranda
Darling or the handsome hero, chasing one another
breathlessly through the chapters. While I leafed, I lost
my grip, and the book fell open on a much-read page:

> He walked slowly towards the old woman in the crowd,
> knowing that her glaring eyes could see right through
> his clothes, to his proud limb … She laughed and
> said, 'You're well-endowed, man-human.'

After that paragraph I turned the pages more slowly.
The paper quality changed, thickened almost, as if the
pages had been soaked and dried again. Slowly the
scene was set for what I guessed was an ancient sex
ritual, and I understood that this was where the hero
took innocent Miranda's virginity:

> The three other women gathered behind him, stroked
> his back and howled like wild animals. Miranda was

under him and felt his erection pulse against her opening. She wanted him now. He broke through the soft
hymen and thrust his fleshy sword into her tight warm
sheath.

I blushed and something unfolded inside me. I couldn't
help but picture, no, *feel*, the hero's huge cock inside
my own shamefully untouched body. I looked at Carral.
She seemed to be asleep in the exact same position,
and I turned back to the book. The sex scene continued
in moans and accelerating thrusts. In the middle of all
this, a line or two before the hero's climax, a sentence
was abruptly interrupted by a shapeless stain. It wasn't
dark and made the type illegible. I put my finger on the
stain: bone dry and naked, timeless. A muscle in
Carral's wrist pulsated, and suddenly it was as if I could
feel that same pulse in the stain, in my finger, in my
crotch.

The book fell to the floor with a bang while I hurried
down the stairs and up to my own mezzanine, undressed
and turned the light off. In the dark the house was so
quiet I hardly dared to breathe, and when I put my
hand into my pants, as if to grab and keep ahold of
myself, I was terrified that Carral could hear what I was
doing, that, through the plasterboard, she might discern
the sound of underwear fabric among the soft rustling
of the sheets. Under the covers, I could still feel my
pulse in my fingertip, in my hip, beating against my

pelvis, and I lay awake. A noise above me made me think of a bird landing and settling in for the night. It would have to be a big bird, maybe a swan, scraping its heavy bird-feet against the metal plates up there. I imagined that it shook its wings and preened its feathers with its beak, and when I fell asleep I dreamed that the long swan neck stretched down past the metal roofing and all the way to me, and that it put its big swan head under my arm, as if I was a wing.

The Spores

THE INSIDE OF THE Earth Sciences building was rounded and painted in earthy colours. The wooden walls in the auditorium curved upwards into a vaulted ceiling. All the chairs, window frames, and desks were variations of green and brown. The inside of the building looked like a well-kept nature reserve. I sat at the back to avoid Dr Spitlip, but today another lecturer had taken his place. He droned on about the development of local spider species. I struggled to pay attention, and in between digressions and slides of fossils, I discreetly read *Introductory Mycology:*

In some kinds of fungi (Rhizophydium) fusion between spores leads to transferral of one parent's genes to the other.

I thought about the stain in *Moon Lips*. It had made the writing illegible and left the page coarse and hard against my fingers.

Later, in the factory, I sat on the mezzanine bent over two small jam jars and tried to occupy myself with local species of spiders and insects. In one jar I had trapped a little white spider I had found on the windowsill, and in the other a reddish-brown earwig picked out of a shrivelled Bloody Ploughman in the compost. The earwig pushed against the glass wall with its scissor-arms, cut the air and rocked backwards, only to try again another place. The spider didn't move.

The wind outside pushed hard against the walls of the factory with a constant pressure, making the joists creak and complain. Behind me I heard Carral leave the bathroom, unbutton the suit she wore at the office and pull her sweater over her head. I looked around and saw her face disappear into the black fabric. Underneath she wore a short vest that nearly reached her tights, and between them her belly showed, like a porcelain enamel plate. I turned back to my jam jars.

'What are you doing?'

'Looking at insects,' I mumbled in reply.

Softer fibres sounded against skin. When she came up on the mezzanine she was wearing tight white tracksuit bottoms and holding a paper bag in her hand.

'We're going out with work tonight. Come with if you like. They're nice people. Some are pretty young too.'

'But isn't that just for your workmates?'

'No no, it's totally casual. And I've told them about you. They'd love to meet *the young Norwegian*.'

I could feel her eyes on me and concentrated on not looking up from the earwig's jar.

'I hope you told them nice things.'

Carral sniggered. 'Just that you're Norwegian and good with rotten fruit. Come on, join us. You'll have to get out and get to know people sometime.' She pulled out her novel and noticed my jars. 'You're doing homework?'

'I'm preparing a lab session, yeah.'

'Are they from the house?'

'I found one in the window and the other in the compost.'

'And how is the compost?'

Her shoulders shuddered slightly.

'The apples are still there.'

Carral nodded and opened *Moon Lips*, put her hand in the paper bag.

'Do you want some *muff*?' she asked and fished out a chocolate muffin. Without waiting for a reply she broke it in half and gave me a piece.

'*Muff*?' I asked. 'No thank you. It's *muffin* though, isn't it?'

'Sure. But we call it *muff*. Have some, come on, I can't sit and munch cake on my own.'

I took a bit of cake. Carral's fingers had left deep hollows on both sides.

'Do you know what muff means by the way?' She giggled while chewing the other piece. I shook my head, and she continued:

'It's slang for vulva. I don't know why. Maybe some people think they look like labia . . .'

Half the cake was still in my hand. I could see the muscles in her jaw moving up and down while she chewed and swallowed. Her toes pattered on the pillows in front of her. In one of the jam jars the small solitary spider had begun to rock, white and tender like a cameo brooch, a miniature Carral.

Later she turned on the TV. From behind the jars I saw the blurry images of a body, and when I looked up, I saw a muscular redheaded man on the screen.

'Do you watch this series?' Carral asked and stuck out her index finger.

'What series is it?'

'*Charmed*. Maybe they don't show it in Norway? Three witch sisters . . .'

'Yeah they do, I don't watch it though.'

'I know, it's *trash*. I like the witch stuff though. You should know the kind of stuff I read.'

I looked down. Carral continued:

'And that guy's really hot.'

The man appeared on the screen again, this time with a woman. She was showing a lot of cleavage and had big inflated lips.

'He kind of looks like Pym,' Carral said. 'Weird, I hadn't thought of that before!'

'Pym? Who's that?'

'Oh, he's our neighbour.'

'Pym,' I said. 'What a strange name.'

'It's a nickname. I think it's actually his last name. Anyway, you'll meet him soon enough,' she said and took another bite of cake while staring at the TV.

Above our heads, at the bar of the Sealion, a happy hour sign blinked in garish pink. I stood among necktie-knots and hairpins that were gradually giving up their hold.

'This is Jo, she's the new girl in my flat,' Carral said to the others, smiling with her nose high. 'She's so young, so young, *little* Jo, only twenty, *young and inno-cent.*' I was about to protest, but Carral just kept talking about me, like you'd describe an old photo of yourself: young and serious, fearless and faded, a frozen moment long past.

'How are you finding the brewery?' Carral's manager asked me, over the blaring music. He was older than everyone else, maybe forty, and wore a suit. I felt his heavy breath and the warmth from his skin against my cheek. *He's a real jerk, and pretty desperate too,* Carral had whispered in my ear. I pulled away a little.

'The brewery?'

'Yeah, the building you live in is an old brewery,' he said, and added, 'at least that's what Carral says.'

'I didn't know,' I answered and looked over to Carral. She'd turned to face a tall, gangly boy.

'The whole Hawthorn district was abandoned for years,' the manager said. 'Until they realised they could renovate the old factories as apartments. That was just a few years ago. Some are pretty nice too. Not for me, of course. I like new-builds. And fresh meat.'

He leant closer again.

'Andrew's sister's in your class,' Carral said and then turned to the tall boy. 'What's her name again?'

'Anna,' Andrew replied. 'Do you know her?'

I shook my head.

'Isn't she the pregnant one?' Carral said.

'Yup. Watch out for biology, *little Jo*,' he said with a nod.

Carral and Andrew laughed.

'Look at my lips.' Carral lifted her head and stuck out her neck as she pointed at them. They had swollen and when she spoke, they barely moved in time with her jaw and tongue. Andrew prodded them.

'Do they have to be woken up?' he asked with a wide grin.

'They're just wasted,' Carral answered, '*sloshed*,' and they both laughed loudly.

'You're not like the other girls,' the manager said.

'Really?'

His eyes were red. They squinted and studied my face. Again I moved back a bit.

'You're not like the girls in the office, or the girls you meet clubbing,' he said. 'You're not . . . like that.'

'Like what?'

'Like . . . skirts and high heels . . . Your hair . . . it's short . . . You're wearing trousers . . . So serious . . .'

'Really?'

'And your face . . . cheekbones . . . They're different . . . Is everyone in Norway so serious?'

His face split in half, his eyes still on me while his lips stretched down for the straw in the drink he held in his hand. His lips covered the straw like a horse's, tightened and sucked.

'Serious, I don't know . . .'

'And your English is so fucking great. Serious and clever —'

'Everyone's taught English at school in Norway.'

I didn't enjoy this conversation, how it focussed only on burrowing deeper inside of me. I felt translucent. Could you tell just by looking if someone is a virgin? I looked around the room to find Carral. She was drinking fizzy wine by the pool table and laughing every time Andrew spoke. Her lips were really swollen, and I couldn't help but think about Miranda Darling's lips,

full and succulent, the envy of her friends . . .

As she took aim, the yellow curls in her ponytail fell over her shoulder to rest below her ear. Andrew bent over her from behind, thrusted the cue, and for a

moment she looked up, straight at me. A paragraph
from *Moon Lips* came to mind:

> He bent over her from behind and parted her legs. She
> supported herself on the basin and moaned as he
> teased her underwear down and undid his trousers . . .

I could feel my palms getting sweaty, and rubbed my
hands against the rough denim on my trousers. The
Moon Lips stain throbbed in my fingertips. I was
surrounded by sex. The scent of salty bodily fluids
flooded the room. The manager had followed me down
the bar, and mumbled in my ear:

'I like girls like you, *your type, you know* . . . *lesbians.*'
He poked a finger deep into my arm. 'Tell me . . . have
you ever . . . been with a man?'

'I'm leaving now,' I said, and glanced at Carral by the
pool table one last time before walking out the door.

The trip home was chilly and my hands were cold and
slippery, but my fingers did not stop throbbing. On the
mezzanine while I waited for the sound of Carral, I
could still feel it. I felt the throbbing against my pyja-
mas and the seams of my underwear, through epider-
mis, dermis and hypodermis.

Then I wake up: there's a smell of musty paper. I haven't
noticed anything, not a sound; it's as if she just appeared
here. This is the first night we sleep in the same bed.

Carral had snuck up here; no questions. There's no hesitation, no reason, no fear. There's nothing. Only springs creaking tentatively and the contours of a hand in the dark.

'Hi.'

Or maybe I'm just dreaming when I hear that.

'Hi.'

Carral's face is silver-white in the moonlight. We're not close. Our bodies watch each other, keeping their distance. We're like two strangers, in different rooms, at different times.

The Brewery

WHEN I WOKE up, CARRAL was gone. The space beside me on the mattress was cold and smooth and the duvet was wrapped around my body like a sleeping bag. There was no trace of her, as if she'd never joined me up here at all. Still I remembered last night in small fragments: the sound of the creaking ladder, the mattress sinking under the weight of our bodies, her warm breath in my hair.

I played music and turned the volume up as high as it would go to push Carral out of my head. In my headphones, noise and effects enveloped a simple vocal melody. Surrounded by the naked factory I got the feeling I was in a church, a sense of space and grandeur, almost dizzying. The vocalist sung with a mysterious, veiled timbre:

Alison, I said we're sinking
There's nothing here but that's okay
Outside your room your sister's spinning

As the song transitioned into an interlude, the melody paled. The echoes of the words remained, as if they had fallen into themselves and continued to be there, smaller and smaller:

Alison, I said we're sinking

I lay surrounded by plasterboard and bricks and felt feverish. When the song faded out, I noticed that the air in the factory had become dense and stuffy. I removed my headphones, stood and climbed down the ladder to the kitchen. The house seemed different, snugger, as if the building had contracted. The kitchen table covered a larger portion of the floor, and the light bulbs swung wide on their cords. Maybe someone had been here, while we slept so deeply, and put a new set of walls up over the old ones, a new plaster layer on the inside of the boards covering our mezzanines. I imagined these things as I walked across the floor to the kitchen counter. My feet trod carefully on the floorboards, as if to avoid bumping into something I couldn't see, but that was still there. It hit me that this was how Carral walked. Had I begun this recently or had I been doing it a long time? I looked down at my feet. They were soft and white on the floorboards, almost liquid.

Carral came out of the bathroom with a towel wrapped around her hair and another one around her torso. I hadn't heard a sound from the bathroom. The toilet wasn't hissing, and the shower head didn't drip. She must have been there ages. The sound of her steps mingled with the sound of the kettle boiling.

'Good morning. Is the bath free now?'

She nodded hello, shuffled past me and disappeared up to her mezzanine. When I went into the bathroom it smelled faintly of urine and the liquid in the toilet bowl was the colour of melted butter. Carral hadn't flushed. When my stream hit the surface it bubbled and as I peed I looked down between my legs and watched the two liquids mixing.

Under the shower head I let the water run so hot it scalded my skin. I imagined I was scrubbing off the manager's disgusting comments and rubbing out Carral's sudden presence in my bed. The shower gel foamed on my skin, a frothy cover between me and the night before, between my body and hers. All the while I saw her behind my eyelids: a soft, blurry face on the pillow next to me, silver-white in the darkness. The water rushed from the shower head, and the sound gained a different, softer quality against the soapy froth that covered the bath. It reminded me of the head on a beer. I forced the image of Carral out of my head and pictured the bathtub, the bathroom, the whole house, as a beer glass slowly filling with sweet fermented hops.

'Is it true that this is an old brewery?' I asked Carral once I was dressed. She looked so tired, almost blurry, sitting at the kitchen table in an old, thin bathrobe. *Moon Lips* was in front of her, closed.

'Yeah, I think so. A long time ago. The neighbour told me.'

'It must have been empty for a long time?'

'Yeah, I've no idea how long, but probably several years.' She closed her eyes and put her hand on her forehead.

'Do you have a fever?' I asked.

'No, I'm just really tired. We smoked a little yesterday; I hardly remember anything. And I slept terribly.'

I nodded. It was quiet between us again, and at once the image of her in my bed returned, her grey face and warm body so close to mine. Carral yawned and stared down into her book. Her index finger stroked the cover, traced the edges around the sketched full moon in circles. My palms were sweating.

'Is it a good book?' I asked.

'Well, it's trash,' she answered. 'But I need it.'

'Trash can be fun.'

'Yeah, but it's a little sad when I think about how I

used to read lots of challenging, gloomy books, proper books . . . And now wolves, mystical powers and love is all that matters to me.' She smiled sleepily and held the book up with the cover towards me, and continued: 'Jo . . . I'm sorry if I said anything stupid yesterday. I didn't mean to call you young and innocent.'

'It's fine. I mean, I am. And that's pretty funny.'

'But actually you're really mature. I heard you dodged the manager.'

'He thought I was a lesbian. He asked me if I'd ever been with . . . a man.' I could feel my face getting hot just by repeating it.

'I'm sorry you had to meet him like that. He was really drunk. But I heard you handled it well.'

'Yeah. But it was gross. He's right though. I've never . . .' My voice became faint. But Carral smiled, leant over the table and put her hands on my shoulders.

'You haven't? *Blimey*, a virgin! I didn't know.'

I looked down. She sat down again and continued:

'But Jo, that's not a problem! That's nothing. We'll find someone for you.'

'Oh no, please don't. Definitely not someone from your work.'

Carral laughed. For a moment she looked almost well. She put her hand over her heart. 'I promise.'

I felt relieved and went to pack up my books. Behind me I heard Carral go up the stairs to the living room. Apparently, she was not working today. When I yelled to say goodbye, she didn't answer. I could see her back leant against the railing, slumped over her book up on the mezzanine. Then I opened the door and took a deep breath, felt the whole great white sky fill my mouth.

Franziska met me at the uni pub after the seminar that day.

'A brewery!' she said.

'Yeah, I wonder how old it is.'

'I went on a tour of the breweries the day I got here. *Brew of the Bourne.*'

'Was it fun?'

'It was horrible. We had to learn drinking songs. I think I remember one.'

Franziska sang a few bars:

> Then come, my boon fellows,
> Let's drink it around;
> It keeps us from the grave,
> Though it lays us on ground.

With her dark voice and heavy German accent the song sounded sombre and serious, as if there was no difference between *the grave* and *on the ground*.

'Should we grab a pint? A few people from the seminar are coming.'

'I've got to go I think,' I answered. 'Carral's kind of tired. I promised I'd cook her dinner.'

When I got home, Carral was sleeping on the pillows on the mezzanine. Her bathrobe had loosened and slipped off her, and through the white cotton fabric of her pants I could see a dark, soft mound, a cress bed of hair. Her cheek was squeezed against the window, her breath fogging the glass. Her skin was flushed, feverish. I leant over her.

'Carral?'

'Hi.'

She stretched, rubbed her cold cheek.

'Still not well? Do you want something to eat?'

She shook her head and pulled the bathrobe over herself.

'Just tea, if you don't mind.'

I nodded and went down to the kitchen, filled the kettle and opened a packet of biscuits. When I returned to the mezzanine with her tea, she'd fallen asleep again. I sat beside her for a while and read my seminar texts, but every time my fingers touched the paper, I thought of the paper in *Moon Lips*, how it was brittle and rough from the big stain. Next to me steam stopped rising from the tea. It cooled and pearls of milk fat spread on the surface. The fluid congealed along the edge and started to sink.

Carral's deep breaths pulled her chest up and released in an even rhythm. With every inhalation her belly, chest, and whole body swelled and collapsed, like a white, slippery dough left to rise. When I eventually lay down next to her, she turned abruptly, grabbed my arm and put it around her.

'Jo,' she whispered, 'are you staying with me?'

'Of course.'

'You don't want to move out?'

Her eyes were still closed.

'No.'

Carral smiled. Then she pressed me close, hard, as if she wanted to pull me inside her.

My arm is around Carral. This is the second night we have slept in the same bed. Through the railing I can see the dim flickering lights from the rotating chandelier by the front door. Then my eyes slip shut and the rays of light become smaller and smaller until the darkness is impenetrable. The whole apartment is slathered with black grease, as though we are in a tarred lung.

In the morning I got out of bed, and went to get milk and toast. Downstairs in the kitchen were several plates with food from the day before that Carral clearly hadn't touched. She didn't want breakfast either.

'But you haven't eaten anything at all,' I whispered.

'I'm full.'

'Full of what?'

'I'm just full-up.'

She was right. Her stomach bulged. Her whole body had swelled in those few hours, and when I snuggled up next to her I could feel how she felt. From her ears I could hear a soft rushing sound, as if from a conch shell. If I closed my eyes, I could hear the house creak and it swayed as though we were at sea. And later in the afternoon, it was as if we were in the sea and carried the house inside us. In my dreams I could feel metal push against my throat and I imagined that I had swallowed the railing, the taps, the window handles, every piece of furniture in the house.

'Tonight, when you feel better, we'll get drunk,' I said.

Carral opened her eyes tentatively and let out a low giggle. 'That'll be nice.'

Then I stroked her arms, her thighs, her belly. Together we filled each other to the brim and lay there slumped in an all-consuming doze, like gorged snakes digesting their prey.

Pym

THAT NIGHT CARRAL seemed a lot better. Outside, the weather was unusually mild, and we sat on the roof terrace for a while, eating crackers and brie and drinking cheap wine from a carton. For every glass I had, Carral had three, and after a while she was pretty drunk and swayed by the TV antenna like the captain on a pirate ship. Behind her Aybourne was a sea of low houses, already in shadow, waves breaking in crests of electric light. She called me over and put her arm around my shoulders, began a sort of wobbly dance and spilt what remained of the wine in her glass. Suddenly we heard a knocking coming from down in the flat. Carral lifted her arm, as if she was conducting an orchestra, signalled for the movement of bodies, wine and clouds to stop, and declared:

'I think we've got company.'

We heard several more knocks. I caught her arm.

'I don't want company.'

'*Little Jo*, it's probably just the neighbour.'

'I don't think anyone should see us like this.'

'Why not?'

'It's dirty here. And we look weird.'

'We are wine, we are cheese, we are crackers.'

'Carral.'

'Come on. You might like him,' she said and looked at me, blinking a few times.

She climbed lurchingly down the ladder humming to herself. Her feet landed heavily on each rung and over the kitchen floor. Her steps were different, clear and heavy, like my steps.

That was how Pym came into our lives, from the apartment next door. He was older than us, in his early thirties, and was the size of Carral and I combined: a tall, ruddy and broad-shouldered man with a whisky bottle in his hand. His hair was thick and red and flattened behind his ears with hair gel. His shirt was half open, thick sun-bleached hair on his chest. He said he was from a small town in the south with waves and farmers and whisky, and that he came to the town to work as a journalist. While in between temp jobs at the *Aybourne Post* he worked on an apple farm in Castlehill and wrote some of his 'own stuff'.

'What do you study?' he asked.

'Biology, but I'm not sure what I'm specializing in yet. I just started.'

'Of course she knows,' Carral said and put her hands at her side, still in a pirate mood. She laughed loudly and stuck up her nose, as if she was balancing something on it. Pym looked at her for a while before his eyes trailed back to me. I didn't want to look at him, and looked down into a spoon. My eye stared back, upside down.

'What are you most interested in then?' Pym asked.

Carral was quiet, leaning further and further back in her chair, and I realised I had to join the conversation. I looked up from the spoon and directly at Pym, who scratched his chin.

'I don't know. I like mycology.'

'Mycology?' I heard him put the stress on *myc*.

'Fungi,' I said, running my fingers through my bangs, feeling a sudden urge to scratch my chin too.

'And you? What are you writing?'

'It's a novel, but in verse.'

'A novel, wow,' I replied.

'Ro*man*, Johanna, ro*man*.' My head sang the Norwegian for novel when I looked at Pym again. He had lifted his whisky bottle and was pouring it into a small shot glass Carral had produced.

'Do you want any?'

I shook my head. He poured some in my glass anyway. His huge freckled upper arm tensed a little while he poured. I wasn't sure if I could stretch even both hands around his arm. He moved continuously, tensing his body and relaxing it again, and I realised that in spite of myself, I was following the muscles in his arms, his neck, his chest. The whisky was sloshing in my wine glass. It was a sticky reddish brown, and had a sharp scent, just like Pym. When I took a tiny sip, I imagined for a second that it came from his body, and it made me cough. When I got up to make some tea, I pictured him grinning behind me.

The sink was full of plates and glasses, dried-up leftovers, mugs and tins. I poked what was left of some baked beans while waiting for the kettle to boil.

'What's your book about?' I asked.

'You can read it if you like.'

'Carral's the literary one.'

'Really?'

'Definitely. You should get her to read it. Right, Carral?'

I turned to her. Her chair was tipped backwards; she seemed to be getting sleepy and was humming a broken tune, making noises intermittently like a dripping tap. I poured milk in the tea and walked over to the table.

'Maybe you'll both want to read it?' Pym leant towards me. A lock of his red hair fell over his face, dividing his eye in two. I hesitated.

'I'm better at biology.'

'This novel is different,' Pym said.

'Really?'

'It's full of nature, full of facts.'

'Hm.'

'I'll let you read it.'

I poked Carral's arm. No reaction.

'Carral's drunk.'

'*Sloshed*,' Carral giggled with stiff lips and without moving.

'I think I should get her to bed.'

'I'm fine, I'll stay here,' she said.

'You sure?'

'Of course! And I want to know more about the book . . . And about what you study.'

'You know.'

Carral leant over the table towards Pym and whispered: 'I think she studies me.'

Her hand was on my arm. I felt her pulse tick in her wrist. Feet arched under the chair. Up on the mezzanine the print of our bodies glowed.

'Is she a fungus?' Pym grinned at me.

'Fungi don't get wasted,' I said. I spoke to Carral. He spoke to me. Carral spoke to the kitchen table:

'Am I myco . . . myco . . . what did you call it?'

'Mycology.'

'My-co-lo-gi-cal?' She forced every syllable, her lips stiff again, and her cheeks flushed.

Then she blinked a few times, and every time she closed her eyes she looked like she was drifting off, a lightbulb about to go out. Finally, she put her head on the table and fell asleep.

The light bulb dangled above our heads, rocking our shadows back and forth over the kitchen table. In the dim light I could see dark stripes in Pym's hair, from the comb's teeth. The walls were blurry and the brewery seemed open like a great hall. On the floor, crumbs sparkled.

'Here, let me show you the beginning of the book,' Pym said and started writing on a napkin. He held a pen between his thick fingers and arched his back over the thin paper. I pictured his back as he wrote, muscles braiding together as he moved the pen.

A few sips of whisky later the napkin was filled with slanted writing. Pym held the pen like a needle between thumb and index finger, concealing the paper with his free hand as he wrote. My hands cupped my tea. He handed me the napkin.

'It's the story of a girl, sort of, in rhyme.'

I accepted the napkin, smoothed it out, felt it stick to my palm.

'It's not finished, though.'

He was apparently a little nervous, because he poured more whisky in his glass and swallowed it in one gulp.

'She', I read, 'creates the world.'

I felt blood rush to my cheeks, salt in my eyes.

The world of biology.
Puts emotion in honey jars with spiders and bees.
Can't see the difference between people and trees.

Through the empty glass in front of him his skin appeared dazzling, as things can sometimes seem, glinting in the distance. I didn't know what to say so I read it again, as though I was struggling with it.

'What do you think?' he said.

'I don't get it. Is this what I'm like?'

'I just wrote what I think.'

'But it could be anyone. Any student.'

'I could have described you as well. Your hair.'

'No, no. No hair. No eyes. No lips.'

I tried to smile, feeling like I'd said something wrong. One word too many: *lips*. The word brought a barrage of thoughts: licking them, biting them, kissing them. I imagined that I bit his tanned neck, and couldn't help but think, *this is it, Johanna, it's happening*, and I was sure he could read it on my lips. His shoulders swelled as he tensed and relaxed his muscles. He leant his head towards me.

'Oh, I see. You're a feminist.'

'That's not what I said, I just think you've written enough.'

'I just wanted to give you a compliment. You have nice lips,' he said, as if adding a coda to the poem, and I squinted back at him, sucking in my lips as though in retreat from his mouth. In my head the words from *Moon Lips* were throbbing:

. . . full and succulent.

I turned to Carral, but next to me I found only an empty brown kitchen chair. She must have gone to bed.

When I look back, I can remember the sound of Carral brushing her teeth, flushing the toilet, shuffling upstairs to the mezzanine while I read Pym's napkin. I remember the sound of a creaking bed and a deep sigh from the other side of the plasterboard. All this returned to me later, as though my senses were slurred, facing Pym by that kitchen table. Because in that moment she was gone, all at once.

Pym and I sit facing each other like two Cheshire cats in the moonlight. He grabs the whisky glass, empties it in one gulp. A drop hangs on his lower lip, a pendulous pearl that remains in place as he smiles.

'You're such weird girls.'

'Oh?'

'Carral looked kind of sick.'

'She was just drunk.'

'And you're a weird one. Cold and pale, like a pearl.'

'You made that up,' I say and get up to signal that he should leave, but instead I walk around the table, stretch out my hand and for a moment I study it in the light, as if my movement surprises me. The hand looks pale, almost transparent.

Then I put my hand on his head, letting my nails trace the comb marks in his hair, all the way to the reddish-blond tips by his neck, his shoulders. I bend over and stick my tongue in his ear, tickling the little hairs on his earlobe, let it slide around his jaw to his chin, follow it up towards his mouth and start sucking his lower lip. It's warm. Then I let go and keep sliding, my lips stroking his day-old stubble. His whole body has warmed at contact and his muscles flex. And for every bit of him I lick and kiss, he shrinks a little before me, as if I'm rubbing him out with my lips, as if his face is disappearing into mine and only the skin remains, white and shiny like the empty sundial in front of City Hall.

Seasnails

THE BREWERY STANK of cigarette smoke, whisky breath and last night's sweat. I stood by the sink and closed my eyes, felt my head burning and tried to imagine that it was the memories of Pym's body catching fire, that he crumpled like paper and withered into a little lump. When I opened my eyes again the air was just as heavy and the memories just as strong. The tap water tasted thick and salty. I imagined the sink filling up with starfish and shells.

'So, what happened between Pym and Jo?' Carral was standing behind me, a glass in her hand. I hadn't heard her approach.

'Good morning to you, too.'

She smiled and prodded my arm.

'Come on. Admit it. You like him.'

I pulled away from her and went to the fridge,

firmly opened the door and took out a carton of apple juice.

'No, I don't think I do like him.'

Carral tilted her head. 'But he liked you.'

'Oh?'

'He was writing for you, and then . . .'

I poured the juice in a glass and took a big gulp to wash away the salty flavour. The juice tasted faintly of fermentation.

'Did you see *what* he wrote though? It was pretty weird, and *he's* pretty weird,' I said and wondered if she could see what had happened reflected on me. My body felt see-through, like a jellyfish.

'You were a little harsh,' she continued.

'And you were sloshed,' I said. 'Pym thought you were ill.'

I took another sip, and the taste brought to mind the rotting apples in the compost. Carral stared back at me and followed the juice sinking down my clear jellyfish throat.

'Come on, I was just drunk,' she said, but for a while she looked thoughtful, and the next time she spoke she sounded hesitant. 'I don't remember anything from after we sat at the table.'

'Me neither,' I said.

In a way, that was true. I wasn't quite sure what had happened after Carral had gone to bed. I remembered Pym's body, the taste of his skin, and my head chanting *this is it Johanna, it's happening,* but nothing else. My body wasn't sore, like I'd read it should be after you have sex for the first time. Everything felt like normal between my legs, no pain. I couldn't find any trace of his body in me, didn't smell anything unfamiliar when I put my fingers under my trousers lining and smelt them afterwards.

Carral and I spent the rest of the morning on the mezzanine in silence. She seemed calmer and healthier than she'd been in days, dipping pieces of bread into a soft-boiled egg and drinking milk from a large glass. Her skin was dry and smooth again, her nipples as usual hidden behind layers of cotton. No more words were exchanged about the Pym episode, but the previous evening was still stuck between us. I looked up frequently and would catch her watching me, and we'd study each other's faces for a brief moment before returning to our books.

Afternoon came. Carral read *Moon Lips* and sucked her index finger. I tried to read *Introductory Mycology*, but kept just staring at the opening pages. It listed fungi parts, reeling them off almost like a nursery rhyme, and while I read the new words I imagined Pym's build: *Fruit bodies* (forearms), *hyphae* (freckles), *mycelium* (chest hair), *chitin* (the firm bulge pushing against me under his jeans), but I couldn't get any further. When I tried to remember what Pym looked like naked, what his dick looked like, all I could think of was a passage from *Moon Lips:*

> She touched his member for the first time. It was silky-soft and stiff at the same time.

The words had been branded into my mind, surrogates for the memory of Pym I couldn't access, a memory that might amount to nothing. And around me the brewery smelled of whisky, sour sweat and Pym's freckled salami skin. The salty taste from the tap water lingered in my throat. It was as if the whole brewery, its walls and pipes, were trying to convince me it had in fact happened when my body wasn't persuasive.

Next to me Carral was trying to separate the pages of *Moon Lips.* She must have got to the part with the stain. Once she'd slid a knife between the pages and they came apart, she turned the page and sighed softly. The article in front of me displayed colourful images of thick mushroom stems and caps, but I couldn't read at all anymore, just sat and listened to her breath, guessing how far she'd got. I didn't notice her moving until her face almost touched mine.

'I think that's him,' she said. 'Should we open?'

Someone had knocked on the door.

'Did I come too quickly?' Pym asked. 'I mean, too early, I mean . . .'

He'd showered and dressed. His breath still smelled faintly of whisky, an odour partly concealed by an overpowering aftershave. His biceps were hidden under a checked shirt. I felt my mouth dry up, my tongue shrink.

'Right now is . . .' I said, but I couldn't continue, and next to me Carral said teasingly:

'*Back for more?*' Then she smiled and continued: 'Just kidding. Of course! Nice to see you. By the way, you have to help us remember last night, because I can't remember anything, and Jo isn't telling.'

Pym hesitated.

'We were just drunk,' I said. My voice was hoarse.

'Yes, that was it, I guess,' he said with a tentative smile. 'I don't know if I have a better version.'

I stared intensely at the ground, but I knew he was looking at me. I could feel his eyes glide over my cheeks, neck and chest. I crossed my arms to cover my breasts.

We went in before him. He sat politely on a kitchen chair and pushed his hair away from his face. My skin felt see-through again.

'I brought this,' he said and got out a rolled-up notebook from his pocket, putting it on the table. His fingers had left shining grease stains on the cover.

'Is this your novel?' Carral asked.

'Yes. It's not that long. It's just a short book. It takes a long time to write verse.'

I didn't say anything.

'Do you want to read it?' he asked and looked over at me, then at the book. His whisky breath intensified, became sweeter, more detailed. *He thrust his fleshy sword into her tight warm sheath* – the passage from *Moon Lips* sang inside my head.

'I don't know . . .' I said.

'Of course,' Carral said.

'It's kind of about you two. Or people like you.'

I looked at the notebook, and it made me sick, just like those vague, waving memories from last night made me sick. My jaw tensed.

'Do I create the world?' I asked.

Pym smiled gently, shrugged. 'It's kind of feminist at least.'

I got up.

'You should probably leave then, so we can read.'

'I guess so.'

He looked a little hurt. A muscle contraction throbbed in one of his wrists, under his skin like a little caged animal, and when he got up from the kitchen chair he looked shrunken. I picked up the book, pulled my fingers across the cover. It was a lot bigger in my hands than in his. The paper was faintly yellowed.

'Thanks, then,' I said without looking up, and when I eventually did look up, I was alone in the kitchen. Carral was back on the mezzanine with *Moon Lips*. Later I got the sense that more had been said before they left, as if something had dissolved and disappeared before it reached me.

Outside the day was paper-white and dry. I walked down the street, stepped over the asphalt under lamp-posts that were blind in the daylight. At the top of the winding silo stairway, I stood by a shattered window looking over at the brewery roof. Inside on the kitchen table Pym's notebook lay, still unopened, and I thought about it as I leant over the empty window frame and spat a warm white glob down onto the street. That was Pym I just spat out, I thought, and that idea helped a little. I kept spitting, trying to form a little puddle on the concrete below. The drops hit the ground with faint splats, and I could hear them humming: '*Pym . . . Pym . . . Pym . . .*' Afterwards I walked to the brewery and looked at Carral, still reading *Moon Lips* on the mezzanine. Her head was so close to the book that the paper grazed her nose when she turned the page. I could see a faint damp stain on one of her breasts.

When I went to get ready for bed that night I'd got my period. I sat on the toilet staring at thick blood clots dripping down into the bowl from my crotch. The blood was old, like it usually is on the first day of my period, and the drops had coagulated into little sticky black lumps. It has always frightened me that I can't stop the blood. It just drips and drips from me to a rhythm I can't control, and now, too, every drip was wrapped in an echo from the porcelain, from the plasterboard, from the firm concrete walls. They whispered to me – *Jo . . . Jo . . . Jo . . . Jo . . .* – as if I was leaking into the room and dissolving, flowing from my own bloody crotch like black juice from a rotten apple core.

Prune Skin

I woke up on the rough floorboards of the mezzanine, having rolled off the mattress. Perhaps the fall woke me. Possibly, I'd lain there some time. I seemed to recall a thump and creak as my body hit the floor, but perhaps these sense impressions were something I'd dreamed up. The sound formed a long, dark and winding stairway of resonance that I fell down. Fragments of the dream I had woken from gleamed around me. The hum from the fridge downstairs sounded like onrushing waves.

When I lay back on the mattress and closed my eyes, my dream seemed clearer to me. I had been looking over the mezzanine wall and down into the kitchen, but it wasn't a kitchen, it was a foggy, beautiful forest with pine trees and blueberry bushes. Between the

trees a group of sweaty male workers had been drain-
ing thick, smoking fluid from the tree trunks into
wooden barrels. It must have been beer. The smell
was heady, and the steam had filled the whole room
and made my skin moist and sticky. Suddenly the
workers had all turned toward me; they all had Pym's
face. They started to sing. Their voices sounded like
the rush of a waterfall. The song stuck to the inside of
my throat, as if it really was liquid, as if I was a beer
barrel.

'Jo,' they sang, 'Jo, Jo, Jo . . .'

'Jo?' something whispered in the dark.

I must have fallen asleep again. Half of me was wet.
The skin down one side was warm and damp.

'Carral?' I whispered.

She was behind me on the mattress, this time close
to me and naked, and I could feel her crying. I turned
around, fumbled in the dark, found her head and
stroked her hair. Her scalp was wet.

'What is it?' I asked.

She didn't answer. Her upper body undulated with
sobs.

First I thought I was soaked in sweat, but when I
woke up properly I recognised the sharp, bitter smell of
urine. A thin, warm stream trickled against my thigh
from Carral's body.

'What are you doing?' I said and sat upright. My top
and pants were dripping wet; my duvet warm, wet and
heavy.

'I can't . . .' Carral whispered. I felt the stream on my thigh become more powerful, as if she had given up trying to hold it in. The liquid trickled in between my legs. 'Can't . . . hold it . . .'

I began to adjust to the light; her contours became clearer. Beads of sweat were glimmering on her forehead, on her throat, neck, hip-bones. Small poppy seeds.

'I'm sorry I came up here. I was so scared . . . and so weak.'

'It'll be OK. Do you have a fever?'

'I don't know. I don't think so.' Her voice was a whimper.

'It's fine. Let's go get changed. We'll have a shower and sleep in the living room.'

'OK,' she said, but remained unmoving on the mattress. I felt her nod slowly with her face in the pillow.

'Does it hurt?'

'No . . . I'm just so tired.'

'Should we wait a bit?'

'Yeah. Till I can get up.' She started to sob again.

So I lay there for a while as the pee soaked into my mattress, the smell of urine intensifying. I continued to stroke Carral's body, first her cheek, puffy and wet, and then her hand. Then I was braver, stroking her naked back, letting my fingers walk her ribs like rungs on a ladder up to her throat. Where everything on Pym's body bulged, as if something under his skin was always trying to tear its way out, Carral's skin was the pristine surface of water. She let me stroke her, lying completely still.

Later I moved close to her side again. Our bodies dried-up like a crystal fist.

'Jo? Could you tell me something nice?' Carral asked after a while. Her voice was shaky.

'What?'

'Anything . . . A story from Norway or something.'

'I'll try. I'll tell you about the toughest girl in my primary school class. Do you wanna hear about her?'

'That sounds nice.'

'She was called Emma,' I said, 'and one time I visited hers, she asked me if I dared get into bed with her naked.'

'How old were you?'

'Seven, maybe? I was in year one. We didn't start school till we were seven in Norway when I was little. Anyway, I said I'd do it, I wanted her to think I was as tough as she was.'

'Were you scared?'

'A little. We undressed and lay down on her bed. And then Emma said that we could get pregnant.'

'By lying there like that?'

'Yeah.'

Carral chuckled softly.

'Did you believe her?'

'No. I knew about sex, but she sounded dead sure. And, in a way, the toughest girl is always right. So I got scared, and I put my clothes back on.'

'Did you get pregnant?' Carral wasn't whispering anymore. I could feel her chest moving against my back in shallow laughter.

'Not that I know.'

When we got up and put all the wet things in the washer, my skin was cold and sticky, like fish skin. Even after showering I smelled faintly of urine. On the sofa cushions, a fidgety Carral in my arms, I wondered why I'd been so scared in Emma's bed back in year one. I thought about how later that same night I had sat by the dinner table with all my clothes on, even my coat. Still I'd felt see-through. I'd imagined that I could feel something growing in my belly, something that wouldn't become a proper foetus, but something much worse: a blackened, dead, and rotten fruit.

The Honey Mushroom

THAT WAS HOW WINTER came to Aybourne: rotting seaweed dried and crumbled to frozen yarn-lumps down by the beach. From the window spot on the mezzanine I saw the car park empty and fill, then empty and fill up again, and the passengers waiting at the tram stop wore thicker coats and more layers. The high street in town was decked with fairy lights shaped like snow crystals. But the snow didn't come, like in Norway and, from where I sat, the window frame seemed more and more like the frame around an old faded photograph: the grass outside yellowish brown, the tree trunks grey and the sky white. Even the laundry on the clothes-horse lost its colours. Once I was certain I'd seen Pym down on the road, but each time he turned toward me his face looked washed out and empty.

As winter settled in outside, we were set upon by summer inside the brewery, as if the walls separated not only the inside from the outside, but divided two different climates. On the floor grass grew along the furring. Yellow moss patches grew from the cracks in the cement. White spiders spun shining fur around the beams and, because of a spreading layer of greenish-white mould, the breadcrumbs on the kitchen counter grew into a little carpet. I tried to trim the tufts and wash away the crawling maggots, but Carral cuddled up against me, took the washcloth and the scissors from my hands, and shook her head.

'That'll just make it worse,' she said. 'I'll tell the landlord, they can hire people from a cleaning company. That's how we do it here.'

But nothing was done, and Carral seemed fine about it. She no longer thought the insects were gross. She let an ant crawl over her hand in peace while reading *Moon Lips*, and she didn't move when one of the white spiders crawled over the hollow of her neck. She just sat there with an index finger on her lips, reading. The next time I looked up from my book and over at her, the spider was gone and her mouth half-open.

I kept going to lectures, and every time I left, it felt like I crossed a threshold between dream and reality, sleep and wakefulness. Outside was cold and clear, and returning to the flat at night was like entering a vast warm cocoon. Carral seldom left anymore. Increasingly she had become part of the damp brewery heat. Her temporary job at Sachs & Sachs had ended, and she had not found a new one yet.

'I might travel instead,' she said when I asked her what she was thinking of doing. 'South. I've saved up some money.' But she stayed at home and made me go to the shop and to the post office to pay our rent and electricity. She would often sit by the window on the open mezzanine, as if she was guarding the brewery and couldn't leave her station. She didn't mention her plans to travel again. But she looked after me too: more often than not, I would wake up with her body next to mine, moist and milky.

It was always her that came to me, but I was always the one left lying awake next to her as she slept. Her curls slipped down her cheek and her skin gently rubbed against the pillow as she snuggled to get comfortable. She would lift a knee and, as it touched my thigh, I'd feel a warm and cold shiver spread from there and out into my whole body. Mostly I would stay still and feel the rhythm of her soft breath on my neck. Sometimes I was sure I could feel little sprouts appear under the skin where she'd breathed.

The plasterboard too produced new summer growth in the house. One day I was in the bathtub, about to fall asleep reading *Moon Lips*:

He let his hand gently touch her soft, swelling lips . . .

Suddenly my hand grazed something that felt like thin soft skin by the bathtub rim. I turned around and looked straight into a white gaping eye: a mushroom, still quivering slightly from my touch, had grown out of the narrow wedge between the bathtub and the wall. The warm spores from its surface melted into slime on my fingers, slipping between the grooves in my skin.

After my bath I warmed some milk for Carral in the kitchen and imagined it was that mushroom in the pot, melting and bubbling.

'Did you see the mushroom?' I asked when I got back to the mezzanine.

'A mushroom? Where?'

She held the milk mug between both hands, gently blowing on it.

'In the bathroom, in the bathtub.'

'Wow, no, it must've grown quickly.'

'Mushrooms grow incredibly fast. They can sprout in a few hours actually.'

Carral nodded and sipped her milk slowly; as she swallowed I felt something warm, slimy white in my throat. I coughed. She turned towards me.

'Don't get rid of it.' She looked serious, and added, 'It's handy evidence of the mould damage, for when the cleaning company arrives, I mean.'

'OK,' I coughed. 'We could see how big it gets.'

'Definitely! Is it edible, do you think?'

Carral giggled. When she dipped her tongue in the surface of the warm milk and licked up the skin, I felt the tip of my own tongue get warmer, and when she closed her mouth I could almost feel the milk skin against the roof of my mouth, like slimy cigarette paper.

Later that night when she came over and breathed on my neck again, I felt the same soft skin melt against mine as I'd felt earlier, touching the mushroom cap. I didn't move but let her envelop me.

The Lighthouse

DEWDROPS TRICKLED down from the beams. The railing was slimy and moist. Carral sat on the mezzanine on a large pile of pillows and watched television on mute, the only sound the hum of the TV set and a brief click now and then when the brightness changed. When I sat next to her, she didn't look up. Her lips were pursed tightly, she looked almost frozen, but when I put my arm on her hand her skin wasn't cold, just clear, as if it had grown thinner. Underneath the pallor I could see pink flesh and a delicate network of veins that glowed in the TV gleam like neon. On the screen I saw a man stand in front of three women, brandishing a long sword. It had to be *Charmed*, because when the man pointed at the women, their faces transformed into red beastly devil-heads.

Moon Lips lay next to Carral. After a while she took it and began tugging at the cover.

'How's university?' she asked, without turning from the TV.

'It's alright,' I answered.

'Are you making friends?'

'Yeah, some. But most of the students are really young.'

Carral opened *Moon Lips*, slid her index finger across the stain on the paper that I'd touched too. Then she put her finger to her face and smelled it.

'Anyone you like particularly?'

'Sure. Franziska, the German one I told you about, I see all the time. Sometimes we hang out with some of the boys in chemistry class.'

On the TV screen the beast-women started to fade, as though a light was being shone through them. Then they disappeared one by one into the man's blade, dissolving in white fog.

'Finally! That's the end of the demon women,' Carral whispered and put her index finger in her mouth.

The man sheathed his blade at his hip and crossed his arms.

'Maybe you should bring your friends here sometime,' Carral said, turned towards me.

'Come out with me tonight if you like, then you can meet them yourself,' I answered and started to collect my things. I didn't expect an answer, certainly not that she would say yes, but as I washed my face in the bathroom later, she appeared behind me wearing a dress and tights, and just said, 'I'm ready.'

On the street I walked first and Carral followed, as if she needed to trace my footsteps. It was the first time I'd brought her out, and the first time in a while that she'd left the flat.

'It's cold,' she said, and shivered a little.

The asphalt felt easy and smooth under my feet, everything was firm and dry out here in comparison with the clammy warm air in the brewery. But even though Aybourne's streets still led to the same places, and the old brick buildings housed the same shops and offices, something felt different that night with Carral. When we crossed the little clearing by City Hall, I saw the sundial, elevated above the crisp winter grass, and the bare pale clock face reminded me of the honey mushroom by the bathtub rim. A few minutes later we walked past the hostel where I'd stayed during my very first days in Aybourne. The windowpanes looked dirty, as though they had grown shut. On the other side of the road was the sea, quiet as ice.

Our walk ended at the student bar. I introduced Carral to Franziska and the other biology students, and she briefly told everyone about herself:

'I have a BA, but at the moment I mostly work temp jobs in offices,' she said. 'It's boring but I kind of don't

know what I want yet. There's just so much that inter-
ests me.'

She seemed amazingly normal in comparison to
how I saw her at home. Curled up on the sofa pillows
in the daytime or hugging me tightly at night. She
seemed more alert and healthy than in the
brewery.

'You live in Hawthorn, right?' Franziska asked
politely. Carral nodded. 'In the old brewery.'

'I didn't think anyone lived there,' Leigh said, a girl
from my genetics class with dark hair and high leather
boots.

'Yeah sure, just not that many,' I said.

'I hear it's haunted,' Leigh whispered.

'Oh?'

'Yeah, my boyfriend was in that house once, before it
was renovated. He said it was haunted . . .'

'Are you saying we're ghosts?' Carral smiled
attentively.

'No, no, but maybe you've seen some?' Franziska
said.

'Apparently a girl died there,' said Leigh, 'the brewery owner's daughter, I think. They say she fell in a tank
and drowned . . . in beer.'

Carral started laughing, louder than usual, so loud
that I ended up watching her.

'I've heard that story too. It's pretty crazy,' she said.

'Tragic, too,' said Franziska, watching me with her
serious German eyes.

'I actually thought I'd seen that drowned girl a couple of times,' Carral said with round eyes. 'But every time it just turned out to be Little Jo.'

She put her arm around my shoulder.

Later I was standing in the bar with Franziska. She'd put on make-up. Her cheeks were red, as though she'd rubbed a Pink Lady apple against her skin.

'You speak differently with Carral,' she said.

'Differently?'

'As if you change accents.'

'I adapt quickly. You know how it is, with *English as a second language.*'

'Yeah, but with her you speak exactly . . . like her.'

'A Brighton accent?'

'Yeah, if that's how she talks. And you act strange. When you were looking at her just now. Are you . . . together?'

'Together?' I asked. A sticky heat oozed thickly into my head and down into my abdomen.

'It's OK if you are, I'm just curious.'

'No, no, we just live together,' I said firmly.

In that moment I noticed Carral, under a big lamp that changed colours at regular intervals. She laughed and squeezed the arms of the chemistry class boys, at first seemingly at random, but later methodically, as if she was in the vegetable aisle, searching for a ripe avocado. And all the while, she looked back at me as she squeezed. Her face was psychedelically gleaming in red and yellow from the lamp.

'I'm sorry to ask,' Franziska said, 'you just seem so close.' She blushed faintly, and stirred her drink carefully with a straw.

'In a way we are,' I answered, 'in that weird house with those paper-thin walls. Sometimes I'm not sure what's going on.'

'How?'

'I don't know how to explain it.'

I felt a heat between my legs. In front of me, red and yellow liquids were mixing in Franziska's glass.

'It's been a while since I kissed anyone,' Carral whispered to me when we met outside the door to the women's toilets. Her hand rested on my neck as she stroked her thumb along my spine. My whole body was throbbing.

'How long?' I asked, but she didn't react, just kept stroking my back, bone by bone.

'Do you like any of the boys here?' Carral asked.

Her lips touched my earlobe, eyes turned towards the group of biology students. I shrugged, and took a step back.

'They're too young for me,' I said.

'They're not that much younger than you, nineteen maybe,' Carral giggled and stared at one in particular, a really tall boy with a long fringe and chest hair that stuck out of his T-shirt.

'That's plenty younger,' I said and walked back to the bar.

Then Pym was there. He stood in the middle of the dance floor with two shirt buttons open and his eyes gleaming. A few locks of hair dangled over his cheek.

'Hi,' he said.

'Wow, you're here,' I said.

'Carral said you were going.'

'Carral? When did you see Carral?'

Pym threw back his head; his hair fell back over his cheek.

'Been a while,' he whispered.

'I've got a lot of reading,' I answered quickly.

'Have you read my book yet?'

'Nearly finished,' I lied.

'And what do you think?'

'I don't know.'

'But you like the idea?'

I didn't answer. He tossed his hair back again, and suddenly he'd put his hand over mine. I hadn't felt it happen, and kept my eyes on our hands.

'It's just for you.' He let go, but his hand remained in the air just above mine.

'Did you see Carral?' I asked again, but I didn't get a reply; in that instant his tongue was in my mouth. I wanted to tear myself from him but his lips were clamped on mine, his tongue filled my whole mouth like a Spanish slug, antennas tickling the roof my mouth. I felt dizzy and tried to catch my breath, but both air and spit was sucked out of me and into his body and in return I got his sticky whisky taste down my throat. His arms grabbed me and held me tight. He closed his eyes. From the outside it must have looked calm, two people kissing each other quietly, but I know what happened inside of me, and I was suddenly afraid to be sucked into him and disappear.

Finally he let me go. I breathed heavily and touched my lips, resisting the urge to spit on the floor. Then I turned around and walked to the bar. I didn't look back. Carral had seen the whole thing from her corner with the biology boys. She had turned her eyes to the bar, but from the tension in her body I could tell she was following my movements. Her fingers had seen what happened, her shoulders, her back and neck had seen it too.

Later that night, Franziska and I said goodbye with a nervous hug.

'Jo, there's a room free at ours, if you want.'

'Why do you ask?'

'Just in case. You said you don't know what's going on.'

She seemed a little anxious.

'Thanks. Can I think about it?'

Franziska nodded and disappeared into the darkness. I looked around, but Carral was gone, Pym too, and I walked home alone with bated breath and steps that seemed to get me nowhere. Soon I saw the silo far off with the rock face behind it, the crag's overwhelming concrete-coloured mouth.

In the brewery, I can see the kitchen over the plaster-board on my mezzanine, with the table like an island in the middle. Behind the table is the ladder to Carral's mezzanine. The rest of her mezzanine is hidden behind a wall like my own. Yet throughout the room I can hear creaking and low voices, muted sounds. I hear them so clearly that I can see what's happening, like an x-ray through the board. I see Pym's thick arms move across Carral's back, envelop her, grip her tight. He puts one hand on her shoulder-blade and the other in the small of her back and she bends over. Then she stretches out and looks right at me, as if knowing that I can see her through the wall, her eyes shining white in her warm reddish face, like splinters sticking out of a compound fracture. Under Pym her spine trembles like a white-tipped mane. The moonlight tints arched joints white, and her tailbone blinks when he pulls her away: a lighthouse signalling the way in the horizon

there, not there,   there, not there

The Storm

THAT NIGHT I LAY with brine in my throat and the image of Carral and Pym together behind my eyelids. My mouth still tasted of Pym's tongue. Neither drinking water nor eating Fruit Pastilles had helped. On my little mezzanine I felt like I was sinking into my own body, into a dark, tight box made of skin and flesh. After a while I fell asleep, and when I woke up a sharp draught hit my face through a crack in the concrete. From the other mezzanine I heard Carral leafing through a book. I wondered if Pym was still there, if they were reading his novel together, if he was touching her. I put on some music, but the song that started playing was from Björk's *Vespertine* album, so intimate it only took me closer to Pym and Carral. The strings and voice sounded like myriads of intimate touches, and each beat sounded like it was played from inside someone's body. I wondered if he was here still, inside her, on the mezzanine across from me. I turned the music off and decided to get up and leave.

The ladder steps from the mezzanine were damp and slippery, like on a quayside ladder. The kitchen floor was moist too, as if dew had formed on the little grass tufts that grew between the floorboards. Lime-stained water drops trickled from the cracks in the wall. And in the bathroom, the bathtub flooded as I showered. The mushroom from the plasterboard was beaded with water, like a shower head.

Out in the streets of Aybourne the gusts were icy. Behind the silo, big grey clouds devoured the mountains and on the other side, sea, islands and sky were tossed together in a great gob of fog and froth. As I leant inwards and walked to the university, I felt the wind pierce every fibre in my clothing, felt sand and dirt gather in the corner of my eye. In the vestibule of Earth Sciences an excitable meteorology professor had hung up a note on the spring weather:

> As always, the forecast is again partly cloudy, with a strong gale coming in from the west. This will shake the dust off those barometers!

Next to the blackboard hung an exhibition of old barometers and the broken arrows veered back and

forth between STORM, RAIN and CHANGE, like an
old seismograph at the start of an earthquake.

While Dr Spitlip lectured on evolutionary theory,
Franziska whispered: 'And then he threw himself at you?'

'Like an animal.' I illustrated with my hands like
claws. 'A MANimal.'

'How gross! Are you OK?'

'I'm fine, thanks. It *was* gross, but he's just some
desperate and pathetic loser.' I smiled and Franziska
laughed in her slow manner.

'Was he the neighbour you talked about? The one
that wrote about you?'

'Pym, yeah.'

Franziska rolled her eyes. 'I can't believe I didn't
see!'

'You didn't exactly miss anything.'

With every word I told Franziska about Pym, he
faded a little inside me.

'I'm sorry that I probed you about Carral,' she said
suddenly.

'That's OK. There really isn't anything between us,
we just live together.'

Franziska nodded and smiled. 'Good,' she said,
'because I saw her kissing someone . . . late, right before
we left.'

'Did you? I didn't see that.' I tried to smile.

'Or . . . it might not have been her. It was dark. And
she was with a big guy.'

'Maybe that was Pym too.'

Franziska laughed, but I thought about Pym and Carral, that it probably had been them, and I wanted to tell Franziska about what I'd seen when I got home, but I didn't quite know what to say, what words to use. Outside the house the world was dry and sharp and normal, and it didn't quite correspond with what seemed to grow between the brewery walls: something moist, skinless and quiet.

When I got home Carral sat by the kitchen table. Pym was nowhere to be seen. She pulled her bathrobe close around her and yawned. Her body seemed to be endlessly far inside it.

'Where did you go last night? I couldn't find you when I was leaving,' she said.

'I was there, with Franziska. Same place. Where were you?'

My face was stiff from my walk through the cold wind, and I rubbed my cheeks.

'In the bar. Pym walked me home,' she answered and poured water in a mug, dropped a tea bag in it with a splash. 'He says hi by the way. He's wondering if you'll be reading his book anytime soon.'

'Did you read it?' I asked.

'Yeah. But I don't remember it so well now.' She fussed over the screw top on a milk carton for a while, twisting it on and off a few times. Then she shrugged.

'No, I can't remember why, but I think you should read it.'

'I'll read it soon,' I said and felt a burning in the roof of my mouth when Carral gulped her first sip of the scalding hot milky tea. She touched her mouth, just as I did. 'Bloody hot!' I heard behind me as I walked to the bathroom door.

In the bathroom I rinsed my mouth out before filling the sink with cold water, and rigorously washing my face. Then I stood and looked at myself in the mirror, poking a finger in my mouth. The roof of my mouth felt normal and cold. But the mirror shook in front of me, and all around me everything was moving; thin rings were forming on the water surface in the sink. The honey fungus rocked by the bath's rim. The grass tufts between the floorboards swayed gently. I turned off the tap and listened. There was a thump that sounded like it came from inside the concrete. When I put my ear to the wall, I heard a soft knocking sound, through the cistern rush.

'Can you hear that knocking?' I called out to Carral in the kitchen.

'Yeah, I think it's Pym. He mentioned he'd be working a bit today.'

I sat down on the toilet seat with my hand against the wall and felt the beating in there, like a tiny heart that grew inside the wall.

The knocking continued through the night with the storm. When I got up to pee in the half-light, I wondered if Pym, assuming he was the one who knocked, could hear us as we heard him, if he could hear me pee, if he could hear the difference between my sharp fast stream and Carral's slow dripping trickle.

The next morning when I woke up it was light and the knocking had stopped. I heard the wind's howl and in the distance ferocious waves broke against the pier. The news told of electricity pylons on the main line that had been blown down, and that power was to be unreliable all day long. Lightbulbs flickered over the kitchen table, the fridge stopped its humming and started again, the TV flickered. The tin ceiling wasn't sealed properly and when the wind caught it silverfish and beetles would tumble down the steel beams.

'We have to get the bins in,' Carral said when I returned from a trip to Aygros. 'They're gonna fly away.'
    'But it'll stink.'
    'We'll put them under the stairs. There's not a lot, just some in the compost, and it's sealed pretty well.'
    The wind almost knocked us off the stairs. Carral carried the bins, and afterwards we each took hold of an end of the coffin-like compost container holding the old apples. The smell of rot on my hands was faint and familiar, and when we put the container down under the stairs I remembered how, when we'd dumped the

apples in it, I had imagined we were cleaning out paradise. I got a sudden urge to open the compost and look at the apples. Carral sat on the lid, and I sat next to her. Her arm was near mine. Her skin was soft, softer than I remembered, as if she was rotten too, a fallen Eve. Under us I could hear the apples rumble. Not a real sound, but a sort of internal buzzing, like how you can imagine hearing nails and hair growing or buds opening.

Goldapple Stems

I WOKE UP DURING the night and saw that the bathroom light was on. Downstairs I found Carral sitting
on the bathroom floor with a fistful of yellow hair in
one hand and a pair of scissors in the other. She
jumped when I opened the door. On her head were
several bald spots.

'It just came off, I woke up and there was hair everywhere . . .' she whispered and sank into a pile of hair,
crying. I sat down next to her and stroked her cheek.
Her head jerked. A yellow lock of hair stuck to my
hand, warm and soft, almost liquid.

'Do you want me to help you?' I asked, and twisted
the scissors gently out of her hand.

There really was hair everywhere. Some locks were
cut, but others looked like they had just come loose
and slipped down her shoulders, gotten stuck in the

folds on her nightshirt or on her arms. It looked like she had hair growing all the way down to the floor, where it fastened. The bathroom mushroom's white eye glared at us.

'I'm starting,' I told Carral, who nodded silently, and then I rested the scissors close to her scalp and cut. The locks of hair fell down in my lap like peelings from a golden apple, and as I was cutting more and more from her naked head, I noticed that I was crossing a line, that I gleaned and gathered something painful from her that didn't fall to the floor, but that braided itself into my body from hers.

When I finished she had only millimetres of hair left, her scalp having become a glistening white button mushroom.

I stroked her head. 'You look lovely,' I said. 'Like a Buddhist priest.'

Carral was completely silent.

I continued: 'Come on, you can sleep over at mine.'

On my mezzanine she whispered in the darkness: 'Remember the time when I lay here and had wet myself?'

This was the first time she'd mentioned it. The words felt strange, as though her voice just decided that it had really happened that night.

'Yeah, I remember,' I said.

'It wasn't on purpose. I'm really sorry.'

'It's fine. I told you that.'

'Yeah, I know. But I just wanted to apologise anyway. There's something in me that makes me . . . lose control sometimes. I fall asleep. And I . . .'

I turned towards her, could only just make out the contours of her face in the dark.

'And what else?'

'I come over to yours.'

'Is that you losing control?'

'No, maybe not.'

'I thought you were scared or something.'

'Yeah. That's it. I feel . . . different.'

'How?'

'I don't know, I don't understand what's happening. It just feels like this is where I should be.'

I turned around with my head facing the plaster-board. It smelled rotten, of wood and mould.

'I saw the two of you.'

'Who?'

'You and Pym, on the mezzanine, fucking like rabbits. You should have told me that's what you wanted.'

'Oh, Little Jo. I didn't mean to hurt you. I didn't mean it . . . I don't really understand how it happened. I only meant to kiss him, and . . . I don't remember much after that.'

'But why?'

'I think I was just . . . afraid to lose you.'

'What do you mean *lose me*?'

'I don't know . . . you'll fall in love . . . and then you'll move out . . . and then I'll be alone here again . . .'

'Move out? I don't even like him! And you didn't need to *fuck* him.'

'I'm sorry, Jo.'

The floorboards creaked loudly when I turned and rolled out of bed. Her arm stroked my back, but I pulled away. My insides were pounding. Then it was quiet for a little while before she whispered: 'But you're saying you don't like him?'

'No, I don't. I just wish you'd told me about it.'

'I'm so sorry, Jo, I'm so sorry.'

'Yeah.'

'Are you gonna move out?'

'Maybe. I don't know. Yes,' I said.

She pulled my shoulder back so I lay down again. Then she turned me toward her, her face against mine. 'Don't go. Come back to me.'

Our foreheads were touching. Two thin crusts of landmass.

'I'm not leaving,' I said.

Later it happened again. I dreamt of Carral's golden hair locks twisting around me like a warm golden exoskeleton. When I woke up, our bodies were clammy and damp. The mattress stank of urine. Warm, thin fluid trickled onto my hand next to her thigh, and I thought about tea with milk and sugar. I could hear the water drip from the ceiling, from the walls, from every corner, and I thought that it dripped with us, for us.

Eden

THE NEXT MORNING the storm had abated, but a torrential rain followed it and the air in the brewery became ever more damp and clammy. Carral was still sleeping when I got up. Her smooth, newly shaved head was beaded with sweat. On the way to the bathroom I felt rainwater drip on me through cracks in the tin roof, and the living room mezzanine was covered with a thin white layer of moss that couldn't be scraped off. I could only barely make out the street below. There were no people, no trams, and I couldn't even see the tracks, as if all of Aybourne had been rubbed out overnight.

The compost was still beneath the stairs. The stench of rotten fruit had spread through the entire flat. It felt like the brewery had been transformed into a big wet tank that was waiting for Carral and I to decompose within it: a rotten, reeking Garden of Eden. The apples were in the bin where we'd left them, mouldy and collapsed. Flies with long legs buzzed around a torn dark-red Bloody Ploughman. The Honeygold next to it had its peel intact, like a shrivelled urine-coloured pearl. Some of the apples were unrecognisable, covered in grey-white fur like little dead animals. And under them, in the far corner of the apple pile, I noticed something different: a notebook, yellowed and soft. I recognised the colour: it was Pym's notebook. Did Carral put it there? I thought while I fished it out and brushed off the worst of the mould stains. Then I hauled the compost behind me through the factory and lugged it to its usual spot outside the front door, chucked the notebook in my backpack and walked towards the university. As I walked it felt like the rotten apples were rolling behind me, braided together to form a sticky yellow-brown trail.

That night I brought the notebook to the bathroom. The honey mushroom sat with its head on the bathtub edge. It had changed colour and was a deep yellow, almost black. While I ran the bath, I sat down to read the book. The mushroom leant against my shoulder and read with me in silence.

Pym's little novel started with the same verses that I remembered from that night around the kitchen table:

The biologist creates the world;
The world of biology.
Puts emotion in honey jars with spiders and bees.
Can't see the difference between people and trees.
Everything she sees she understands;
Everything can be made from her hands.

It wasn't a long story, and I read most of it before the tub was full. It was the mythical tale of a girl, a biologist, whom I guessed was supposed to be me. The girl met a man, who of course reminded me of Pym:

His body so tight, his arms so strong,
His hair as red as fire.

The biologist had created the world, but she had also created another girl – who had to be Carral – and the whole thing ended in a strange sex orgy where the two girls took turns at satisfying the man's every sexual fantasy and eventually melted into him:

They thought him strong, he thought them pale.
They covered him like a long, white veil.
And so he saw the world through her eyes,
The world that she created.
THE END

I splashed some water in my face and shook my head. Was this really how he saw me? Did he want me to

show him a different world, or did he just want to have
a threesome with Carral and I? I went to close the book,
but noticed little prints on the paper. I turned the page.
On the flip side of what I had thought was the final
page were several more stanzas written in completely
different handwriting:

> But wait! This story isn't over yet,
> Another scene has just been set.

And then Pym's book continued with a short grotesque
feast:

> The women feast on the poor man's flesh,
> And chew each bone whilst it is fresh,
> So the two women can become one with a kiss;
> The dream of every biologist!
> To grow together is their pursuit,
> And his red flesh their forbidden fruit,
> He stumbles and gasps and finally dies;
> From his ashes will a four-breasted creature arise.

I recognised the handwriting from notes and shopping
lists. Carral's. I shut the book and squeezed my eyes
shut, trying to push the final lines out of my head. But
behind my eyelids the images returned again and again,
as I dried my hair, brushed my teeth and snuck out of
the bathroom: Carral looking straight at me while Pym
thrust himself in and out of her body, Pym's tongue

burrowing into my mouth, Franziska saying, 'You seem so close,' Carral giving me a muffin, sitting next to me on the compost lid, peeing down my thigh.

There she was, in the middle of the kitchen floor outside the bathroom, waiting for me. It was dark now and there was no light on, so I couldn't see her face, just the silhouette of her body shining in the glints of light from the chandelier. She moved towards me on slender legs that stuck out under a nightshirt, silent and jagged, a deer sneaking tentatively into a clearing.

'Jo? Have you been in the bathroom this whole time?'

'I guess.'

I held up Pym's book to her and continued: 'Did you write the last page?'

'Oh, Jo, it was just a joke.'

'A joke?'

She laughed lightly.

'Almost all of it. And some of it . . . for you.'

'For me?'

'Come.'

That was the first time I was on her mezzanine, and when she turned and lay behind me, firmly against my body, I thought we were synchronized, or I wished we were: that she should dream what I'd dreamt, that she should taste what my mouth tasted. And in my mouth I felt two tongues, mine and hers, licking each other's lips and swallowing each other's spit.

Her breasts push gently against my backbone. I can't feel her nipples, just smooth skin, and where the nipples are supposed to be there are instead two small holes. From these two holes grow two thin stems that burrow through my skin and flesh, twisting and tangling around my spine. Along my back little yellow fruits start to grow. I feel their taste in my mouth: cold sweet sap.

Then there's a rush through me, her stalks and fingers and veins spread through my entire body like a new soft skeleton.

Black Fruit

THE BREWERY WAS QUIET, the kind of quiet that resembles sleep. Carral twitched like a dog that dreams of running. Every twitch pinched my skin, and the last thing I thought before I disappeared into sleep was that sleep is an animal, an animal body. And then I was gone, unconscious: paws and claws grew out of my fists, fur spun out between my legs and wove around our bodies.

I dreamt of two bodies, girls' bodies, our bodies: our upper bodies had melted together and our necks twisted around each other, thin and long like swans' necks. The girls were naked and hairless. The faces were shadowed. It was impossible to tell who was who. The cracks between them were covered in white mould fur, as if they shared a skin woven around them.

One of the girls turned her head towards the other and said, 'Let me tell you a fairy tale,' and the other girl nodded. So the first continued:

'I'll tell you the fairy tale of the apple. Eve ate the apple, and then Adam came and did so too. Afterwards the apple was forgotten, and it was assumed that it rolled away in the grass while Adam and Eve were chased out of the garden. But that's not true, because secretly the apple rolled in between Eve's legs, scratched open her flesh and burrowed into her crotch. It stayed there with the white bite marks facing out, and after a while the fruit-flesh started to shrivel, and mould threads grew from the edges of the peel. The mould threads became pubic hair and the bite mark became the slit between the labia. Soon all of Eden followed the apple's example and started to decompose and rot, and since then this has happened in all gardens and everything in nature, and honey mushrooms came into existence, and rot and parasites and beetles arose. But the apple was first, and it never stops rotting, it just gets blacker. The apple has no end, just like this fairy tale.'

While the girl recounted the story, a forest grew around their two bodies, a forest that at once was and wasn't the brewery. The pine tree crowns burrowed through the roof, a waterfall splintered the stairs from the mezzanine, the floorboards melted into yellow and green heather, and then it started to rain, a mild autumn rain that whipped the girls' bodies soft and smooth. A deer walked out between the trees with an apple in its mouth. It had Pym's face.

'Jo?' Carral's voice rang.

I opened my eyes and saw that I was still on the mezzanine. The heather in my dream was grass, the grass that had grown in between the floorboards. Carral was glued to me, and I thought of the girl-bodies in the dream, how they looked like fantasy creatures, and remembered the last sentence that Carral had written in Pym's book:

From his ashes a four-breasted creatures arises.

Carral whispered, 'Do you remember the tough girl I told you about? The one I lay next to naked?'

'I told you that story,' I said.

'What? No, I remember it happening. I can't have been more than seven, and I was at Emma's house, Emma with the plaits. She had bunk beds. We were in the top bunk, naked.'

'That's right, we were in the top bunk, I remember, but that's my story.'

Now I was confused.

'I remember being so scared of pregnancy, even though I knew it was impossible. The rest of the night I wore all my clothes,' Carral whispered.

'Yeah, I even buttoned up my coat. How did you know?' I asked.

'Let me finish the story,' she continued. 'That night I dreamt of a snake hidden under my bed, a snake that could sneak up under my duvet and in between my legs.'

'And I had to fold the duvet and put my legs around it . . .'

'Like a kind of protection.'

'I thought: anything can inseminate me now,' I whispered, 'anything can get into me.'

'I know. That's my story too.'

'How?'

'I don't know, but I can hear you.'

Her hip-bone stuck to my thigh. I moved my leg, but as our bodies slipped apart, I heard her body make a sound, not a normal sound, a fantastical sound, something like the sound of a nail breaking, of a bone fracturing, or flesh being torn apart. I closed my eyes and imagined damp dark beads rolling from her finger flesh, out of her mouth, her hip socket, vulva.

Carral continued: 'Imagine if the world was like Pym's book.'

She was so close that her damp breath wet my earlobe as she spoke.

'You mean *your* book, like what you wrote in the book.'

'Yes.'

'In your book the tough girl would've been right,' I said. 'People would have grown together just by lying next to each other.'

When I closed my eyes, I thought that we really were in Pym's book, and asked Carral, 'What happened with Pym that night?'

'I don't know, Jo. I don't remember that much. Just that Pym came in with me, and that I read his book while he was there, and then he was gone, Jo, he wasn't there, and I was awake, and it was day. And I felt so sick, as though I'd devoured him, and the book, and everything that happened.'

'In your book you would've done.'

I imagined Pym and Carral as I'd seen them through the plasterboard wall that night. I saw their naked bodies, Carral's white skin and Pym's red face. And now I could see things I couldn't see then: Pym's tongue dissolving and melting like cotton candy in Carral's mouth. Carral's body opening and devouring him, slipping over his body and covering it like a thick, soft dress. I saw this in my head with eyes closed and I saw it when I opened them, because on Carral's skin I could see little freckles, Pym's freckles, pushing back and forth,

there, not there, there, not there.

Her eyes were closed, and when she opened them she put her arms around me. I whispered to her, 'Everything can come into me now,' and she answered, 'I'm coming.'

I want to tell her that I'm scared, that this is too much, but instead I put my lips on hers like she put hers on his that night: I bite and suck them, chew and gnaw, suck Pym from her and into me, blow him back into her in big, clear bubbles where I can see our faces mirrored, Carral and Jo, two sets of lips sucking the same man in and out of each other's mouths. Here lay two Siamese twins, bound together by a thick freckled masculine sinew. And when something pushes in between my labia I'm torn and I scream, blood trickles down my thigh like warm dark fruit juice. Whatever's in there twists in all the way, crawls up to my black apple and bites, and that's how we are bound together:

Carral and Jo,

Carral and Jo together:

A black, dead and rotten fruit.

Afterwards Carral rests on my shoulder blade, hip-bone, femoral neck, backside of my knee. From the roof, from the walls, from all corners, I can hear the sap dripping with its silver-shimmer echo, and I think that it drips with us, for us, from us, and that I have to leave.

Together we sleep like unicorns.

Under the Sea

THIS IS HOW I REMEMBER my last day at the brewery:

I open the front door with my suitcase in my hand and I can't find the world outside. No town, no view, no lights and no islands. No asphalt or concrete buildings, no dead trees. Nothing. No air. Only one thing exists: a foggy darkness so thick I think it's a dark wall of water pushing against my hand, threatening to submerge me, as if the house is the cabin of an old ship sinking into the sea.

Carral is awake. I've run a bath for her. She says, 'Stay here a little longer. Just one night.'

'OK, one night. But tomorrow I'll be gone,' I answer.

'Are you sure you want to leave?'

'I have to.'

She cries, and sobs the same words again and again: '*Little Jo.* Stay with me.'

Her voice follows me like a yellow beam of light when I cross the kitchen floor and up the stairs to the landing. The chandelier trembles, and the glass stalactites are dripping. I sit by the living room window and study my own mirror image. Glowing blue-white lips. Behind them I see the dimmed shadows of Aybourne's streets and towers.

I imagine the city under water: only a few church spires, silo pipes and the City Hall clock tower reach the surface. The roofs continue into the sea in broken lines, mirror images seen from below. On the other side of the brewery the mountainside disappears into the water's surface, and the silo organ pipes gurgle, barely above the salt water. The ocean floor is covered in white, a layer of matte limestone made from billions of white spiders – no – bones and skeletons from forest animals and tenants – or is it beer foam?

Inside the house there's still air, but the walls are dark, soaked with water like a treasure chest. Water drips through the keyhole. And slowly, so slowly that I almost don't notice, the sea covers the grass tufts on the floor like a glittering salt carpet and starts rising while it whispers:

> Full fathom five thy father lies;
> Of his bones are coral made;
> Those are pearls that were his eyes;

Nothing of him that doth fade,
But doth suffer a sea-change
Into something rich and strange.

The same was whispered to me about Carral, about her skin, which will become apple peel, and about Pym, who melted into cotton candy on her lips.

At the same time I imagine the tide ebbing and flowing over us, and the foamy waves breaking against the silo pipes. Through the night the words Carral wrote in Pym's book fade in and out of my mind. The lines write and then erase themselves in front of me. I sit and listen to the waves. I brush away barnacles from the window. Maybe the sea is already within this house, as it covered all of Aybourne millions of years ago. Perhaps that's why it's so hard to breathe, and my body feels light, as though it's floating. Maybe we have been living among ghosts all this time, the shipwrecked and the brewery workers. I never saw them, only Carral.

Carral sleeps in the bathtub. Her eyes are closed, mouth open. Under her white skin I can still see Pym's freckles and Pym's cheekbones. Pym's red eyes flicker behind her eyelids. Inside her mouth I see the honey fungus, like a rotting black tongue. She lifts a hand, grabs my jumper and pulls me down towards her, and I pull back. Tide, tide, don't come here!

Carral? I'll finish your fairy tale. You forgot to mention the snake. In the story the apple poisons the snake, and Eve packs her books and moves out of paradise. *The End.*

This is how it has to end, so I carefully pick the honey fungus out of her mouth. Then I bend over and put my lips on her lips:
    first I draw Pym out of her,
       the scene from the mezzanine,
          and the kiss in the bar
            I draw out the night by the kitchen table.
Then I draw the nights in my bed out of her,
    Our legs twisting together,
       Eve and the apple,
         the story of the hardened girl:
And then I blow,
       I fill her body with air until not a single trace of Pym, or me, remains.

I'm leaving now, Carral.

Then everything starts rushing around me, as if I've pulled a plug, as if all the saltwater is being drained out of the beer barrels, the bathtub, the house. Carral doesn't open her eyes.

I cross the bathroom floor and open the door. I stay standing there for a while. Then I go outside. When I walk down the street, it's a struggle, as if I have roots in the house that are stretched long behind me, and no matter how far I go, no matter how many corners I turn on the way to Franziska's flat-share by the beach, they are stuck. They stretch, get thinner and thinner until they are as fine as thread. Slowly but surely I imagine that the brewery crumbles and follows me, threading itself on my cord as though it's a house built from small gleaming beads. The front door reaches me first, then the floor panels from the kitchen, the enamel from the bathtub and the steel covering from the taps, glass-splinters from the chandelier and the apple cores from the compost. And Carral follows too. She crumbles in the bathtub. Tooth by tooth, nail by nail, bone by bone. And new beads grow, threading themselves on my roots. The beads appear from her mouth and eyes, her crotch, hip socket and fingertips.

Epilogue

I IMAGINE CARRAL behind me that day, while I pack clothes and books. She stands by the windowsill as if she is on a long quay. Her body is wrapped in faint white fog, blurring her silhouette. I barely remember her, and I imagine that she could be gone at any moment, swallowed by the fog, but she remains in the same position. Later, when I don't hear from her and try in vain to find her name online or in phone books, I imagine that this is a moment I've duplicated again and again, like a scratched record, but right now the moment lasts so long I worry she'll disappear. If she would just turn her head, blink, shift her weight from one leg to the other, but she doesn't. The silk dress clings to her body in the wind. Everything is quiet, so quiet I later forget why we came here, why we are here.

—

Only the wind moves her. And then she is gone.
  There,   .

When I write this, I think that there are two versions of
myself and just one managed to get out, first out of the
brewery, then out of the town, out of the country, back
to Norway. The other is still there, with the other ghosts
in the house, shut in while the storm and the sea tears
at the walls outside.

I bend over this white sheet and pull her out, the one
who is left in the brewery, pick her up from the bottom:
      Arms,
            swollen fingers,
                  broken skull,
                        burst lungs.
Her face is white, covered in lime, algae skeletons, beer
froth, and sea foam.

I stroke her head, smooth and bare and shining: a glistening doorknob without a door.